Sheri Chapman

Chief Spirit Bear
Rise to Power

A Passion Series Story

By Sheri Chapman
Cover by Rachel Olsen

Chief Spirit Bear

This book is a work of fiction. Names, characters, places and incidents are products of the author's imagination and are not to be construed as real. Any resemblance to actual events, locales, organizations, or persons living or dead, is entirely coincidental.

COPYRIGHT

Trient Press

3375 S Rainbow Blvd

#81710, SMB 13135

Las Vegas,NV 89180

Ordering Information:

Quantity sales. Special discounts are available on quantity purchases by corporations, associations, and others. For details, contact the publisher at the address above.

Orders by U.S. trade bookstores and wholesalers. Please contact Trient Press: Tel: (775) 996-3844; or visit www.trientpress.com.

Printed in the United States of America

Publisher's Cataloging-in-Publication data
Chapman, Sheri

A title of a book :Passions of the Heart

ISBN

     Paperback: 978-1-953975-08-9

     E-book: 978-1-953975-09-6

DEDICATION:

I want to thank my agent and publisher, M. L. Ruscsak for always supporting and encouraging us. I appreciate all her hard work to get our products out there. I also want to thank a great friend and my biggest Passions fan for inspiring me and keeping MY passions alive for this line of stories. My original plan was for a trilogy, but she is strongly encouraging me to continue the series. If I do, please send thanks to my wonderful inspiration, Cara Kwek. <3

<u>CHAPTERS:</u>

Chief Spirit Bear

Bear Power: Sixteen Winters
Sixteen
Calm
Seventeen
War Chief: Seventeen Winters
Eighteen
More Respect

Chapter One
Curiosity

The orange flames softly licked the bottom of the logs. They swayed against blue or red partners, switching quickly and without reason as the song popped and teased in the background. As the melody became more powerful, the orange ladies pirouetted in yellow skirts, twirling this way and that. Gentlemen dressed in blue finery tossed them to red men who melted back into blue. The performance was alluring.

A pregnant blonde was naked, nestled in a bed of the softest furs. The backdrop of fire framed her silhouette in a romantic light. The woman was made of gold: her skin was touched with the color, her honeyed tresses curled with a golden sheen, and her eyes were pools of liquid amber contained in almond-shaped molds with pieces of emerald swimming freely in them.

A strong, bronzed hand lay protectively across her swollen abdomen, lovingly massaging her stretched skin and teasing the child who lay kicking beneath. Firelight danced along the war chief's muscles, outlining and defining each. Shadows rippled along his supreme body as he moved his hand in a circular motion, calming the restless one inside.

"Our *hoksicala* does not like to be woken in such a way, my wife," Spirit Bear said in amusement.

She giggled and said, "I do not blame him, my chief. I am sure his world was quaking."

Spirit Bear arched his head back and laughed heartily. "No wonder he is kicking so much," her husband agreed.

For a few more minutes, they basked in the quiet warmth of the morning, smiling when their baby gave another vigorous kick against his father's hand. Kaitlin reached up and traced her husband's pectoral muscles. Her face was thoughtful and inquisitive.

"What was your life like as a child," Kaitlin asked her husband, "as a chief's son?"

"I feel that *Wakantanka,* the Great Spirit, has always smiled upon me," Spirit Bear responded. "I had a blessed childhood and had every advantage of a warrior-in-the making. My father and his best friend, *Wawakankan's,* father, were inseparable, much like I am with my hearth brother."

"Was *Wawakankan's* father a spiritual man as well?" her pink lips were parted in the wonder of her question, and her cheeks, flushed from their recent activity, complemented her golden complexion.

Spirit Bear's hand stilled over another strong kick. He smiled, kissed her stomach, and said, "He was not a shaman, *hiya,* but he was very naturally gifted in the spirit world. *Wawakankan,* or Wonder Worker, inherited his natural gifts, and he trained under our old healer before he passed."

"Is that why he is the band's medicinal advisor?" Kaitlin asked.

"*Tos,*" Spirit Bear said. "Wonder Worker is very skilled and learned twice as fast as any normal person, so his knowledge was vast when Wandering Elk passed. The tribal council felt he was ready, so we voted to honor him as shaman."

"That's really interesting," Kaitlin said, her eyes expressive. She only waited a heartbeat before softly asking, "How was it with *you*?"

Spirit Bear was thoughtful. His black eyes met hers, and he answered, "When I was nearing nine winters, I was chosen to become a warrior."

Kaitlin held her breath. Then she asked, "That is not usual, is it, *wastelaka*, my love?"

"It is not uncommon for the young boys from a man of known warrior status to be watched for potential," Spirit Bear replied. "But one is not usually groomed as early of an age as I was. Normally, our men do not become village leaders until they are around thirty winters."

"Is it because you were a chief's son?" Kaitlin hung on his words, hungry for more.

"I believe partly, *tos*. There is no honor higher than telling a man that his blood child is the best and has been chosen early for the warrior elite," Spirit Bear admitted, "The council had watched me from the time I could walk. When they suggested I begin training at eight winters, my father could not have been prouder!"

Her husband leaned down and placed another kiss on Kaitlin's stomach. She smiled on his intoxicating features, her love shining in her face.

"Do you wish the same for our son if he is born a male child?" she asked.

"Of course, *tos*. There is no higher compliment," Spirit Bear said with a smile. "Any son of ours will be watched for prowess. It is likely he will inherit the grace of an elite warrior because he comes from a line of war chiefs."

Kaitlin stared at his full lips and nodded. She was silent for a time. The fire continued its melody, and the chief swirled his hand over her belly in loving circles.

"Will you tell me more?" she finally asked.

"If that is your wish, *tos*. The weather is bad this sun, so we will stay inside unless our attention is needed," Spirit Bear said. "I will tell you my tale."

"Oh, thank you, *wastelaka*!"

He nodded once as only a chief could and began his tale. "In the Bear Claw Clan of the Oglala, boys who are seven winters old begin to learn how to use a bow and arrow. We stress the importance of tool construction and how to use it safely. Once they master the care of their weapon and shooting, the boys begin to learn stealth and tracking."

Kaitlin took in a small, surprised breath. Her golden orbs were wide with wonder. It seemed like such a young age to be exposed to the violent side of their lives. The blonde was mesmerized, wanting to know all about the structure of the community she was now a part of.

Spirit Bear used his hands to gesture toward his weaponry and continued, "In our world, if a man does not master the art of silence, he is dead. A warrior must walk on quiet feet to kill or escape an enemy, and a hunter must not make noise if he wants to eat."

"*Tos*, I understand why boys must begin so early," Kaitlin agreed.

"It takes many years to hone their skills," Spirit Bear agreed. "Boys at eight winters may also begin learning to use knives and other war tools."

"They begin to fight one another at eight winters?" Kaitlin asked in surprise. Her golden orbs were wide with wonder.

Spirit Bear smiled. "It is not a typical thing, *hiya*. Most males begin to participate in mock battles and fight against one another in training when they are closer to twelve winters. Up until then, they merely learn how to handle and care for their weapons, how to wrestle without tools, how to make war swipes, and such."

As Kaitlin listened to her husband weave the tale of his youth, his story came to life. She could envision the young boy her husband used to be.

12

Chapter Two
Warrior Training Begins:
Eight Winters

"Son, *uwa yo*," Chief Takes Chances said to his eight-year-old. "Although you are young, you are no longer a boy. Are you ready to be a man?"

"I have much honor, Father, in being chosen," his son replied. At this time in his life, Spirit Bear was known as Red Hawk. "I am scared, though," he admitted.

Red Hawk was a lithe young man. He was tall for his age and well-built. His stance was straight and tall, and he handled himself like a proven warrior already. Many in the band treated him as if he were older, probably due to his physical maturity and emotional stability.

"That will never go away, *Cinks*, my son. It is good to have fear in your heart but not in your actions. It will keep you alive."

"*Tos*, Father."

"Come. We train."

Chief Takes Chances was in charge of war raids, so he was also the man who trained boy-warriors. When the youth of the band had mastered basic hunting skills and wrestling peers in competitions, they were typically between eleven and twelve winters. Then they would learn more precise techniques in the art of war under the direction of the master.

The war chief would assort the groups primarily by ability but sometimes by age. The boys began learning the fundamentals of fighting with wooden knives. From there, they would learn to master other weapons. Lastly, before entering warrior status, they had to excel at killing techniques.

All young boys learned how to use weapons after they could hunt. However, not all became warriors. If the man had not entered into warrior status by his seventeenth winter, he typically became a hunter by default.

Only the bravest and most daring of men were given the honor of serving on the *Cante Tinza*, or Brave Hearts. This society of warriors were the men with the highest coups. When a difficult raid or defense move was needed, the *Cante Tinze* carried out the tactic. It was a dangerous society to be a part of, but all warriors wished to have the honor.

Red Hawk followed his father to the training grounds. He stood proudly as his father waited to announce his presence to the other trainees. Inside, however, Red Hawk was quaking. He was sure some of the older teens would resent his youthful intrusion.

"Listen, young warriors," began Chief Takes Chances. "I know you know my son, but you may not be aware that he's been chosen by the Tribal Council to begin warrior training."

One boy, Snake in the Grass, obviously wasn't pleased with the revelation. He dropped his weapon with the announcement, momentarily attracting attention. He was in the age bracket of the oldest boys-in-training. His eyes were narrow and squinty, and his unfriendly face was punctuated by his terse, thin mouth. Immediately, Red Hawk could sense the rage emanating off the small man-boy upon his arrival on the training fields. Quickly, the youth masked his expression and picked his item back up.

Red Hawk was not discouraged by the teen's standoffish manner. It made him more determined to beat him and earn his respect that way.

Chief Takes Chances placed Red Hawk in the youngest group, and quickly, his focus switched. The concerns about the older boy dissipated.

In addition to learning with older peers, Red Hawk also received individual training from his father. Chief Takes Chances taught his son how to assess the body language of his foes while in battle in order to predict their deadly moves. The leader also taught Red Hawk tricks he'd learned through his own experiences. The youth was a sponge and mastered moves after only a few times of practicing them.

It wasn't long before Red Hawk began to fight other boys. Since none were of his age, the eight-year-old learned with peers at least two years his elder. Red Hawk was a natural fighter and quickly rose in the ranks. He was beating men much taller and older than he was. There was something in the way he moved. It was as if the spirits spoke to him and conveyed what his opponent was going to do. It made Red Hawk nearly impossible to beat.

Wonder Worker was also a boy of eight at the time. His child name was Straight Arrow. He was in the process of learning how to fight and hunt. Basically, all boys, beginning at the age seven, had to start training so that they could hunt and provide for families later.

"That is excellent marksmanship," Straight Arrow said as he admired the still-quivering arrow in the very center of their target. The red hawk feather guides were perfectly placed on his friend's weapon.

"Thank you," Red Hawk replied. "You also shoot well."

"Not as well as you, but I am good enough," Straight Arrow replied.

"Do you want to surprise our parents? We could hunt and bring back fresh meat for our meal fire this night."

"That sounds like fun!" Straight Arrow said happily. His face erupted in a smile.

They boys melted into the greenery.

Gentle Rabbit approached her friend's hut. "*Hau*, Bubbling Brook!"

"*Hau*, Gentle Rabbit! Come in! I just made dandelion root drink. Would you like some?"

"*Tos*, thank you. What is on your agenda for this afternoon?" Gentle Rabbit asked, accepting a steaming cup.

"I need to gather fresh vegetables for my meal, for one thing," she replied.

"Let us do this together. Will you join us for our evening meal?"

"Am I not there most evenings?" Bubbling Brook said with a laugh. "Are you sure you do not wish a night to yourselves?"

"I have every night to myself when you leave," Gentle Rabbit added her laughter to her friend's. "We are one big family. I love sharing meal time with you."

"We would be happy to come!"

The women finished their drinks and grabbed some baskets to collect the fresh vegetables. When they returned, their baskets were brimming with assorted dock leaves, wild garlic, and onion root. They'd also gathered a few other fresh roots and edible plants that were ready during the season.

"I will prepare the cook fire and begin the main meal," Gentle Rabbit said.

"I can help you," Bubbling Brook suggested, "or I will make a dessert, if you'd like?"

"Yes! That will put a smile on our men's faces," Gentle Rabbit agreed. "As well as mine!"

The women turned to their self-assigned chores. About then, two adolescent boys appeared silently in their yard.

"Oh, you startled me, you noiseless young men!" gasped Bubbling Brook.

The boys' smiles grew wider. They held something behind their backs.

"Look, Mother," Straight Arrow said proudly. Both boys swung their prizes into sight. "We bring meat for our dinner!"

Gentle Rabbit and Bubbling Brook gasped in exaggeration. The boys proudly held up three rabbits and four grouse.

"Look, Bubbling Brook!" Gentle Rabbit exclaimed. "We no longer have children in our huts!"

"You are right, my friend! They are truly hunters! Now we must feed four men, not two!"

"Thank you, our sons," Gentle Rabbit said, her eyes soft with pride. "Your prowess for your age is commendable!"

"You brought home plenty, Straight Arrow and Red Hawk! Would you mind to pluck the birds while we skin the rabbits?" Bubbling Brook asked.

"*Tos*, Mother, we are happy to help," they replied in unison.

Red Hawk took the leather bag partly filled with feathers so they could add to the collection. Bubbling Brook and Gentle Rabbit retrieved the rabbits. They would work together to skin the animals before beginning individual dishes.

The rabbits were seared with a seasoning of crushed garlic and salt-brush solution. Gentle Rabbit turned the meat regularly, and the fat dripped onto the hot rocks below. The liquid sizzled and quickly evaporated, saturating the air with the smell of savory meat. The aroma inspired grumbling from all the stomachs of those waiting from around the pit fire.

The batter of the *Aguyapi*, was perfectly mixed. It contained rehydrated fruit from last year's growth. Gentle Rabbit poured a small amount on the hot rocks beneath the rabbit. It would not stick and the fat coating the stone would absorb into the baking flatbread. More scents wafted into the air.

After the *Aguyapi* finished, Gentle Rabbit stirred the grouse soup and removed it from the fire.

"If that meal is not ready before long," Wind Walker growled appreciatively, "I will have to eat it anyway."

Takes Chances laughed. "It smells very good!"

Right when Gentle Rabbit took the meat from the fire, Bubbling Brook arrived with a dish of dessert. She had made a creation with rehydrated prickly pear.

The women dished the meal on to the plates. Instead of filling two plates, they filled four. Gentle Rabbit took two plates as did Bubbling Brook. Before handing it to the men, they stopped in front of their husbands and spoke.

"This night, we serve our man-child with his father. They killed and helped with the preparation of the meat. For this, we will honor them as they are soon entering into manhood," Gentle Rabbit said.

"Do not expect this daily," warned Bubbling Brook, laughing. She made direct eye contact with the young men. "This is a recognition of your *approaching* manhood; this door you have not yet walked through. We are proud of your skills, and for your first time providing for our evening meal, we honor you."

The motherly women handed the plates to the males seated around the campfire. Bubbling Brook filled cups and handed them to Gentle Rabbit to distribute, and then they filled plates of their own.

"This rabbit is delicious," Wind Walker said. "You boys killed rabbits in their prime. Good job!"

"The grouse soup is also delectable," agreed Takes Chances. "The bird is tender and flavorful. The soup is really good."

Red Hawk and Straight Arrow smiled in pride. They were very happy to make their folks so delighted.

"This meat does taste exceptional," Straight Arrow whispered to his hearth brother with a lopsided grin. Red Hawk nodded his agreement with his mouth full of the steaming meat.

Chief Spirit Bear

Chapter Three
Snake in the Grass

"Young men," announced Chief Takes Chances. "Today you will partner up and track one another. Your job is to ambush your 'foe'. One of you will leave to be tracked by the other. You will wait for the hunter's attack and parry it with one of your own. Use wooden knives and any skill you can to take down your opponent. Pair up now!"

Red Hawk was well-liked enough by his peers, but most of these older boys were not in his normal friend group. In addition, most who had pitted themselves against the younger male had also suffered a loss. Although they were proud of the chief's son for his progress, no one cared to be humbled and lose coup when pitted against him. Therefore, sometimes Red Hawk had difficulty finding a partner.

Two of Red Hawk's closest friends were training to become warriors, but they were a couple of years older than he was, and they'd already paired together. The only other young man in need of a partner happened to be Snake in the Grass, the boy who resented his very presence.

Blue Jay and Sturdy Oak teased their younger friend with facial expressions, quick smiles, and suggestive brow wiggling when they saw who Red Hawk would be up against. The two teens were best friends with Red Hawk and Straight Arrow, but when it came to pairing up while they were still not yet men, it was always Blue Jay with Sturdy Oak. While engaging in games, Red Hawk always paired with Straight

Arrow, but since the other was not yet training to be a warrior, it was not possible to be his partner. Later, all four men would eventually serve on the Tribal Council. Blue Jay would come to be known as Sky Warrior, and Sturdy Oak would be Lone Wolf.

Since his best friend, Straight Arrow, was not available, Red Hawk allowed his feet to take him in front of Snake in the Grass. Although the sixteen-year-old was smaller than average in stature, he still stood a good foot over Red Hawk's substantial size for a boy of eight. The teenager's eyes narrowed in anger and his tongue darted out to moisten his thin lips.

"Expecting to win, Son of the Chief?" he sneered.

"I hope to," Red Hawk replied calmly. "It is the plan for both of us, is it not?"

"Do not expect me to give you favorable treatment like the others."

"They do not treat me differently," Red Hawk stated.

"Bull. They let you win for favor of the chief. How else would one such as you win?" he scoffed.

"I will show you how," promised Red Hawk. His black eyes focused on his opponent and read the fear underlying the other's words. He added, "I will not dishonor you."

"If you win, I *am* dishonored, so that will not happen." Snake in the Grass's nostrils flared.

"We shall see. There is no dishonor in losing when we learn," Red Hawk soothed. "There is only shame in one's actions."

Snake in the Grass sucked in a breath and he laughed dryly. "You have much to learn, Son of the Chief."

Red Hawk only smiled as they waited for his father to return.

Chief Takes Chances finally stood before them. "Are you ready?" he asked after giving them the wooden knives.

"*Tos*," answered Red Hawk.

Snake in the Grass simply nodded, staring down his much younger adversary.

"Snake in the Grass, you go first. You've been training a while, so you should be good at covering your tracks. See if you can elude my son. Go!"

Snake in the Grass left at a run. He would wait until he was out of sight to pull tricks out of his hat.

"*Cinks*, are you ready?" his father looked down proudly at him.

"*Tos*, Father."

"A word of advice. Be ready for anything this one has in his bag. He is not an honorable loser. He is also not so skilled. You will find him right away. This is his last few months at training to be a warrior."

"He will not make the cut?" his brows lifted slightly with question.

"*Hiya*. This is between us, Red Hawk." Chief Takes Chances laid a hand on his son's shoulder.

"*Tos*, Father." He nodded once to reiterate his comprehension.

"Do not gloat. He has a fragile ego."

"I will not dishonor him," Red Hawk promised. His eyes met his father's with a genuine promise.

"Good. Now *go!*"

Red Hawk followed the path the older boy took until he was out of sight. At first, it was difficult to discern where the other may have gone. The training grounds were a more highly traveled place, so well-trampled earth did not relinquish clues easily. Finally, he made a decision and began to track.

Red Hawk could see what his father meant. The boy was sloppy. The young warrior could tell his opponent was trying, but he simply hadn't learned the basics of concealing his trail.

Did Snake in the Grass have trouble learning, or did he just not pay attention? His life would be over his very first mission if he was allowed to become a warrior. Red Hawk had considered allowing the other to have some pride of evasion for a time, but that would lead to false hope. He made the decision to attack upon discovery.

The older boy's trail led to a stream of fresh water near their village. *At least Snake in the Grass knew that water could conceal the hunted.* The gurgling, icy brook would mask noise, erase footprints, and even cover up lingering scent.

Still, Red Hawk knew exactly where his adversary was. He crouched, waiting, just over the steep bank carved in the soil. Silently, the young warrior stalked forward.

With a practiced war cry, Red Hawk jumped over the embankment and landed right at Snake in the Grass's feet. The other boy cried out in alarm, but he'd prepared for discovery. He'd fisted dry sediment and fine particles from the creek, and as he jumped in fright, Snake in the Grass threw the sand in the younger boy's face.

Red Hawk's eyes were filled with the eye-damaging filth. He spat and shook his head, but it was to no avail. Snake in the Grass took advantage of the other's predicament. He pounced on his foe's back. He had his wooden knife ready to slash his throat.

Although the younger warrior was distracted by his painful eyes, he was a natural predator. He relied solely on his instincts to save him. When Snake in the Grass gleefully jumped on his back, his reaction was to reach up, grab the other's head, and flip him over. The older boy had never seen such a reaction and was totally unprepared.

Snake in the Grass was lying on his back when Red Hawk made the killing swipe without being able to see. After earning his coup, the eight-year-old made his way to the water's edge by feel. The young warrior bent over to cup water up to his eyes when the second attack came.

With an angry growl, Snake in the Grass jumped on him again. His intentions were not honorable. Due to his opponent's larger size and weight, Red Hawk was propelled forward into the water. He felt his feet give way from beneath him. Snake in the Grass's knees were in the middle of his back, pinning him, and his hand on the back of his neck held his head under water.

Red Hawk floundered in the water, trying to unsettle his rider. Before he really had time to react much, the weight on his back was suddenly gone. Strong hands lifted him from the watery domain. His friends, Blue Jay and Sturdy Oak, were looking at him with concern.

"I can see!" he said happily.

"We pull you from the water, concerned that you cannot breathe, and you say you can *see*?" asked Blue Jay with concern. He quickly did a search over him to make sure he wasn't injured further.

"Maybe he is oxygen deprived," stated Sturdy Oak, more to Blue Jay than to either of them. "He may have been under the water longer than it looked."

"Did you hit your head?" Blue Jay asked.

Red Hawk flashed a smile at his friends and then searched for his adversary.

Snake in the Grass sat on the bank, shivering, obviously concerned with what would happen to him once the war chief found out what he'd tried to do. Red Hawk walked over to him flanked by his taller, more menacing backup.

"Snake in the Grass, you are a poor sport. I do not think you are worthy of warrior status. I won, and when I tried to remove the sand from my eye, you jump on me? You are dishonorable!" For a child not yet into double digit years, his voice resembled a cold and deadly threat.

Snake in the Grass said nothing but continued to look down.

"Highly dishonorable!" snapped Blue Jay.

"I was not going to hurt him," said Snake in the Grass, "but I should not have jumped on him." His words were mumbled, as if they were hard for him to utter.

"No, you should not have," Blue Jay agreed.

"Not only did you jump on him," Sturdy Oak said, "but it looked as if you were trying to hold him under the water."

The three older boys continued to stare at him as if they were one. Still, the other did not look up.

"I would not have hurt him," the sullen boy repeated. His brows inched lower in scared defiance.

"On top of that, you threw sand in his eyes and still got coup counted against you?" Blue Jay asked, incredulously.

"The chief said to use any way we could to take down our foe!" Snake in the Grass snorted in defense. Finally, he dared to glance up.

"The chief said to use any *skill* to win," Sturdy Oak corrected. "Throwing silt in one's eye does not require skill."

Snake in the Grass's stormy face darkened even more, but he didn't reply. He looked away in irritated shame.

"I will not tell my father what you did in front of everyone. I do not intend to dishonor you more than your actions already have," Red Hawk said, "but a warrior would not have acted so."

His two friends agreed; they, however, were still very angry with their older but smaller peer.

"You do not know what you would do if your life was at stake," muttered Snake in the Grass darkly.

"We know what we would *not* do," Study Oak disputed.

"Let us go back, now," Red Hawk said. He felt himself growing weary of trying to speak with one who would not listen.

The three friends led the way, followed by a resentful and scared Snake in the Grass. Immediately, Chief Takes Chances noticed his son's dripping clothes and eldest boy's level of saturation and demeanor. He took the trainees to the side.

"What happened?" the leader asked. His tone was disapproving.

Snake in the Grass's head hung. The other three boys didn't say anything. They thought less dishonor would come if they allowed the guilty one to admit to what he'd done.

"I was not a good sport," the older boy finally acknowledged.

"What did you do?" the chief asked. He faced the sixteen-year-old.

"I used a tactic that these two do not think was fair," Snake in the Grass said with a nod toward the two tall boys. "I threw sand in your son's face."

"So you defeated him through trickery?" Stands Tall asked.

"No," Snake in the Grass said.

"No?" The chief's brows raised. He paused and then asked, "And why are the two of you wet?"

"Even though he could not see, your son still counted coup against me, and I got angry."

"What happened?" the chief repeated. Only Red Hawk noticed the miniscule narrowing of his father's eyes.

"When he stooped to get the sand out of his eyes, I jumped on him," Snake in the Grass admitted.

When it didn't look like he would say more, Blue Jay said, "He helped him stay under the water until we pulled him off."

"I was not going to hurt him," Snake in the Grass immediately denied.

"*Cinks*, is this true?" Those serious, onyx eyes of his father's settled heavily upon him.

"*Tos*, Father. He jumped on me and pushed me under, but I do not know of his intention. My friends came quickly and pulled us out of the water."

"Training is over for this sun," Chief Takes Chances stated firmly, looking up briefly. "Go home and dry yourselves." The leader turned to Snake in the Grass directly and said sternly, "Think over your actions. When you return, I expect you to propose a way to gain back some of the power you lost today. Go."

Red Hawk was thankful to get out of his wet clothes. Spring temperatures were nice in the hottest part of the day, but it was still too cold to go for swims and wear wet leather for any length of time.

That night at the supper fire, Wind Walker, Bubbling Brook, and Straight Arrow joined them. They brought dishes of food to add to what they were cooking.

"I heard what happened," Straight Arrow said quietly to Red Hawk. "Of all the luck, you had to get stuck with Snake in the Grass for a partner?"

"*Tos*, it was not fun. My eyes are still scratchy," Red Hawk admitted.

Wind Walker spoke to Takes Chances, "My *kola*, friend, do you mind if a guest joins us this night at our meal fire?"

"All friends of my spirit brother are *kola* of mine," the chief responded with a slight pat on Wind Walker's back. He turned to the women and said, "Bubbling Brook and Gentle Rabbit, please prepare an extra plate. We will have a guest this night."

"I sure hope he did not invite Snake in the Grass!" Straight Arrow whispered vehemently.

"No, he would not," agreed Red Hawk.

"Who will be joining us, my husband?" asked Gentle Rabbit.

"He comes now," Wind Walker responded.

The band's shaman, a highly respected elder who also served on the tribal council, was slowly but steadily approaching.

"It is Wandering Elk!" Gentle Rabbit exclaimed. "It is an honor to feed our shaman!"

The women filled the men's plates to brimming. There was fresh antelope tenderloin and watercress salad drizzled with thickened meat broth. There was warm *Aguyapi* to accompany, and filled horns of water.

Once the respected elder was seated, the women flew in with the loaded plates and distributed them to the men. Next, they filled the boys and their own plates.

"It is an honor to have you join us at our meal fire," Chief Takes Chances said.

"It is my pleasure," Wandering Elk said, "Thank you for the invite!"

The shaman and Wind Walker were close friends. Wind Walker was a natural at communicating with the spirits, but he didn't have the knack for healing that the older man did. Still, Wandering Elk often asked for Wind Walker's assistance on spiritual healings and preparations. For this reason, Wandering Elk often joined them at meal fires.

"I come tonight to formally ask you and your son a question," said Wandering Elk between bites. His features crinkled with a white smile, and his dark eyes flashed joy.

"The very thing we discussed for the past moon?" Wind Walker asked. His returned smile was full of pride.

"*Tos.*" The elder nodded once in affirmation.

"Let us finish our meal, and then afterwards?" Wind Walker suggested.

The old man smiled, nodded once again, and put another bite of steaming, tender meat into his mouth. The rest of the party ate in silence. Their eyes would dart periodically to the elder in curiosity, but otherwise, each tried to feign interest. It was for the one bearing the news to reveal when he was ready.

In record time, everyone had eaten his and her fill. The women collected the plates while the others chatted around the fire. When they'd returned from washing the dishes, the shaman stood.

"Straight Arrow, would you join me?" The old man's features were stoic and serious.

The boy looked surprised. His wide eyes met Red Hawk's, but neither knew what was going on. Straight Arrow stood tall and proud and then approached the esteemed elder by the fire. When he reached the Medicine Man's side, he stood expectantly.

"Do you know what a healer does?" Wandering Elk asked, looking down on the young man.

Straight Arrow looked into his eyes and replied, "You save lives, Shaman. You ask for spirit guides to help heal those who are ill or hurt."

"*Tos*, that is part of what I do," Wandering Elk smiled approvingly.

"My father sometimes assists you," Straight Arrow added.

"*Tos*, I do ask him for help with the more involved situations," Wandering Elk agreed. "Do you know what else we do as a medicinal leader?"

"You collect plants to heal others. You prepare the vegetation as medicine or poultices and use them on people who seek help."

"*Tos*, very good," the shaman beamed with pride.

The elder said nothing for a few minutes. No one else wished to break the silence, and Straight Arrow tried his best not to fidget or shift his weight under the adult's scrutiny.

"Your father tells me of your interest in learning about plants," Wandering Elk said with a slight inflection: it indicated a small question where he'd voiced a statement.

"*Tos*, I am very interested in learning about healing," Straight Arrow admitted.

"And Wind Walker also says he hears the spirits talk to you and about you as well."

Straight Arrow's eyes widened even more, if that were possible. Finally, he nodded.

"I have come to ask if you would honor me by learning from me. I need to share my knowledge with one who is gifted who can perform the ceremonies as they are prescribed, and one who shows interest and an aptitude for learning medicinal plants. It is a very serious profession. What plants you mix for medicine, if prepared incorrectly or in the wrong dose, could kill instead of heal. I only want the perfect student for what I ask."

Straight Arrow's demeanor brightened. "I would be very honored, Shaman!" he exclaimed. His excitement shone through his attempted calm.

Wandering Elk clasped forearms with Straight Arrow and then with his father, Wind Walker.

"When would you like him to train with you?" Wind Walker asked.

"I still wish him to train as a boy his age with his peers. He needs to know how to hunt and war. He can come to me after his sun's training has ended."

"Every sun, Wandering Elk?" Straight Arrow excitedly asked.

"You need time to also be a boy," the elder wisely replied kindly. "I will train you every other sun. It will give your learning time to absorb and also give you time to play and train with your friends."

"You are very wise, Wandering Elk," his father laughed. "Thank you for this highest of honors!"

"I am happy to finally have a man to follow in my tracks!" Wandering Elk replied with warmth.

Everyone settled back around the fire. The men smoked a pipe and shared stories, the women finished cleaning up and brought out sewing or basket work, and the boys were left to talk.

"Congratulations, my *kola*!" Red Hawk said. "I am very proud of my hearth brother!"

"Thank you, Red Hawk! It is a high honor! I am proud of your warrior path as well! Never has one at such an age as you been chosen!"

"*Wakantanka* truly blesses us," agreed Red Hawk. "Let us go tell Blue Jay and Sturdy Oak!"

The boys scampered off to find their friends.

"What will you do about Snake in the Grass?" asked Wind Walker after Takes Chances had told the tale of what had transpired earlier in the day.

"I will bring it to the next council meeting before our induction ceremony. He is not fit for warrior status."

"You must never take your eyes off of that one," Wandering Elk advised. "He will bring trouble upon our band in the future."

"I also feel that he is not well in his mind," agreed Wind Walker.

"What will he do?" Takes Chances asked.

"The winds of change may come upon him, so it is not for me to say. Our futures are not set in stone, but most do not veer from their path. Just warn your son that he will be a thorn in his future and to not trust that one."

"I think he may already be aware of this after today," the war chief said flatly, "but I will warn him further. I will also watch Snake in the Grass more closely."

"He has shown himself to have a vindictive heart," Wind Walker said. "Will he hurt anyone as a hunter?"

Wandering Elk said, "Not at this time. Again, be wary of this boy in the future."

"You will be our band's new shaman someday?" asked Blue Jay incredulously.

"*Tos*! Wandering Elk asked me to train with him at our meal fire this night!" Straight Arrow's face was vibrant with excitement.

"Congratulations, my *kola*!" the two other friends said at once. "We are very proud of you! What an honor!"

They took turns slapping Straight Arrow's back and laughing together in shared camaraderie. Then they occupied their time playing games together and enjoying time away from the seriousness of man training.

The council met on the day before the ceremony to discuss those coming-of-age and to consider which of the new men to inducted into warrior status versus who would join hunter ranks. At this time, the council consisted of six men. There were two elders, three middle-aged men, and one somewhere in between.

Chief Takes Chances was head of war; Chief Storm Cloud was the community leader; Chief Tracking Dog was in charge of large hunting expeditions; Wandering Elk was the shaman; Wind Walker had a hand in helping the shaman; and the last member was the eldest. He was a very wise man and had lived many winters. For this reason, Sees All helped to council the Bear Claw Clan.

As always, the ceremony began with a cleanse. The men stripped and stoked the fire, throwing incense onto the flames. Once the council lodge was hot, they smoked the peace pipe and each drew into himself to meld with the spirit world. Upon return to the physical state, they would don their buckskins and smoke more of the peace pipe. Then they would begin with the business on the agenda.

"There are three young boys who are sixteen winters," Chief Storm Cloud said.

"They are of an age to be made men. Yet, that is a bit old to make a good warrior," Sees All stated factually. The lines on his face deepened as he contemplated his words.

Most who went to warrior status were made men earlier than sixteen winters. The common age was fourteen or fifteen. At that point, they still continued to train but as fully-fledged men who had achieved the necessary standing. Those not yet chosen for fighting were inducted as sixteen-year-old hunters.

"We agree," said Chief Takes Chances. "We gave them many opportunities to show skill, but they are sloppy. They should show more potential than they have. It is as if they do not care."

"Perhaps they do not," agreed Wind Walker.

"Snake in the Grass does not want to lose coup, so I do not think he chooses to lose," Chief Takes Chances stated dryly. "He showed this when he tried to drown my son."

"What is this?" asked Chief Storm Cloud. His face was genuinely surprised, and a frown hinted at the edges of his mouth.

The war chief relayed what the three boys had revealed upon their return from the river.

"Red Hawk was drenched from the river, and so was Snake in the Grass. He does not show the temperament or the skill for a man of war. One must have his wits about him which means he must control his temper."

"He is one we will need to keep a close eye on in the future," reminded Wandering Elk.

Sees All agreed, "The signs are there. He may hunt, but even with that, he has a poor skill base." He paused and said, "and he's had the best teacher. He just does not seem able to learn."

"He is smart," warned Wandering Elk. "Maybe not the most skilled in his mind, but his intelligence is good enough to think of trouble. Time will reveal his true nature. Until then, we watch."

Wind Walker said, "He does not seem to have friends. His family stays to themselves and does not contribute to the band much."

"They do not have abundance," agreed Tracking Dog. "The father's skills are poor as well, but he is able to feed his family. It will be good if Snake in the Grass can help provide."

"We agree that the three older boys will join the hunters, then?" asked Chief Storm Cloud.

All in the council nodded. They continued their discussion of the proposed ceremony for several hours. When they needed a drink, they would pause, stoke the fire, replenish the incense, and smoke more.

Chief Spirit Bear

Chapter Four
Revelation

"Snake in the Grass is really Snake Strike!" Kaitlin exclaimed, struggling to rise onto her elbow.

Spirit Bear smiled and stroked his wife's honeyed locks back from her face. "Relax, *wastelaka*. He is no more. He cannot cause any more mischief, but yes, Snake in the Grass's adult name was Snake Strike."

"He was venomous!" she cried. "He tried to drown you? And you were only a boy of eight!"

"*Shhh*, my love. If my story upsets you too much, I will continue it at a later time. I do not want you so upset. Our child was just going to sleep, and now he is active again," Spirit Bear said with a smile. "Lie back, and I will get you a drink."

Spirit Bear got up, retrieved water from the intestinal skin, and poured it into a horn cup. His wife watched his lithe movements. He was like a graceful panther. His muscles rippled under his bronze skin, and he was as silent as a shadow. It added to his overall male beauty. When he handed the vessel to his wife, he smiled tenderly at her upturned face.

"Thank you, my love." Her breath was airy and light. She added, "You are so handsome!"

After she drank her fill, he placed the cup to the side and kissed her.

"If you keep looking at me so, I will insist on taking a break from telling of my upbringing," his full lips twitched in humor.

"Please, *Wonya Mato*, I want to hear more! I will not get upset! Your life is so interesting. I want to know what our son may experience as a child of the war chief. Only you can tell me this story!"

"You agree we are having a son, now?" Spirit Bear laughed deeply, the rumbling came from down in his chest.

"It is possible," she admitted, grabbing his hand. "We could still have Sunflower, but you can tell me a story about a little girl's upbringing later."

Her husband laughed again, his humor making her heart swell with love and joy. Kaitlin treasured how their two hearts beat as one. They could lovingly tease one another, work together, go their separate ways to do chores, play, and most of all, she enjoyed how they loved one another, both physically and emotionally.

"Please, my love, tell me more. I will always think of Snake Strike as a coward, but I will try not to get upset," Kaitlin said with a slight frown marring her expression.

Spirit Bear tapped her nose gently and said, "Snake Strike taught me a valuable lesson, *Mazaska Zi Ista*. If it weren't for him, I'm not sure my skill level would have risen so quickly."

"I am sure you are wrong about that," Kaitlin responded, "but why do you say such a thing?"

"He taught me that you can trust no one but your very closest friends. I trusted that a man of our band would not harm me, even after I'd counted coup against him. I did not have a chance to get out from under him in the waters before my spirit brothers lifted us out of the creek, but I realized that no matter who you are up against, most do not lose well. When I had turned my back on Snake in the Grass shortly after my victory, he saw an invitation for revenge."

"*Woniya Mato*, you were only eight winters!" Kaitlin exclaimed.

"It does not matter. I was a warrior-in-training," the chief said seriously, "It could have been my last mistake."

"But he was sixteen and had thrown sand in your eyes!" she argued.

"Do you not think that a desperate man, fighting for his life, might not resort to something similar? One must be prepared for anything while fighting for life," the war chief explained.

"But he was Oglala!" she sputtered, nearly unable to comprehend the huge dishonor the man had committed, "And he was *not* fighting for his life!"

"*Mazaska Zi Ista*, in a sense, he felt like he *was* fighting for his life. He wanted to be a warrior more than anything, and that sun was, in essence, his last attempt," Spirit Bear paused and smiled tenderly at his captivated wife.

"Did he not think of his consequences if he would have drowned you?" Kaitlin cried.

"*Hiya*, my wife. He would have worried about his consequences later. I will tell you more, but know that the life of a warrior is not all full of cherry blossoms. Parts of my story will upset you."

"*Tos*, my chief. I will try to stay calm," Kaitlin agreed. Still, she couldn't help muttering, "At least Karma got him!"

The comely blonde settled back into the luxuriant furs and snuggled close to her husband. She looked up into his sculpted features and admired him for the millionth time, thankful he was hers.

Spirit Bear's defined arms rippled as he closed them about her body and pulled her closer. When he resumed his story, Kaitlin quickly plunged back in time as if she was remotely watching his life as it unfurled.

Chapter Five
An Induction Ceremony

The drum beat resonated throughout the clearing that was surrounded by the entire population of the Oglala village. The chieftains were in full ceremonial dress as they greeted the newly-birthed women. After announcing their adult names, the females joined the other women so they could help with the final preparations of the coming feast. They would dance their womanhood tribute right before the banquet. Then, as part of the Bear Claw Clan's tradition, they would serve succulent foods to their leaders after the boys-to-men section of the ceremony.

The drum beat changed, indicating that the women celebration was over, and it was time to announce the new men. The fresh rhythm was enthralling. Kettle and base drums beat a tempo that the wood and bone flutes enhanced. Bone and gourd rattles punctuated the melody. The happy people smiled and swayed.

The buoyant music led to the adolescent dance of those about to announced as men. In an organized but frenzied step, they circled the fire. Their feet were a flurry of stomping and winding movement. They twisted and turned, waving their arms with power. Their voices uplifted praise to *Wakantanka*. For the many that watched, the sight was awe-inspiring and full of hope.

After the dance, the boys lined up before the chieftains. There were ten males being inducted into manhood. Each boy-to-become-a-man was introduced independently. When Wandering Elk called the boy's child name, that person stepped forward.

As the community watched, his training and accomplishments were announced by Chief Storm Cloud and Chief Takes Chances. Then the boy would announce his new name revealed during his vision quest. The community would repeat it back, indicating that his child tag was gone forever. Wandering Elk would slip a *wanapin* around the new man's neck that symbolized his upgraded status and reflected his revealed totem.

Before the new adult left the natural clearing, the hunting chief or the war chief announced which group he would be considered a part of based on his performance during his child-training. The rest of the council would do an honorable arm clasp and then the young man left the stage to roars of support from the crowd. This continued as each man was inducted.

Snake in the Grass had to be aware of what was coming. He appeared sullen during the whole ceremony. The celebration was the largest, most important event he'd ever be expected to participate in. It was a time to rejoice and be proud that he'd finally reached manhood status, but Snake in the Grass was proud of nothing. He was the kind of man who blamed others for his misfortune, looked through negative eyes on every experience, and played the victim card to the fullest. There was no making him happy.

At last, Wandering Elk cried, "Snake in the Grass, please come forward."

The resentful teen walked forward as pridefully as he was able and stood before the chief.

"Have the spirits revealed your man name?" he asked.

"*Tos*. I am to be called Snake Strike," he replied. He nervously licked his lips. He was not used to having every eye upon him.

Wandering Elk brought forth a wooden *wanapin* with an ornately carved snake on it. The snake formed an S with its body, its mouth was open in a hiss, and small fangs were visible. It contained a few beads and stones of green and brown. It was a pride-worthy gift.

Snake Strike leaned forward to receive his totem's mark. Wandering Elk placed the *wanapin* over his head, and the necklace felt heavy on his chest.

Chief Tracking Dog stepped forward and said, "It is an honor to count you among the Bear Claw Clan's hunters." They did an arm clasp.

Before he left the center of attention, Snake Strike clasped the arms of all members of the Tribal Council. Although he was thrilled at the recognition he'd received and the honor of the *wanapin*, Snake Strike was still upset that he had not been chosen to serve as a warrior. When he reached his family, he turned to watch the rest of the celebration, but a little more ire was added to the black brew in his heart for the chief's son.

Next, the new women performed a shy and mildly seductive dance for their community and for their leaders. Then they retrieved the plates and offered the food to each member of the Tribal Council.

Once the men began eating, it signaled the rest of the community that the feast had begun.

During the eating festivities, music continued and all warriors who wanted to compete entered into a tournament for a coup feather reward. Any rising warrior would be a potential candidate for a future induction into the *Cante Tinza*: the council would be watching.

Chapter Six
Admission

"My life really changed when my parents disappeared," Spirit Bear said after a small break in his story. He took a long drink from the horn cup of water.

"Do you want to talk about it?" Kaitlin asked. She reached out and touched her husband's warm skin. She ran her hand down his muscular arm and could feel the tension vibrating under the surface. "If it is too difficult to recall, you do not have to tell the story. I know it was hard on you."

"If you want to hear about my rise to power, then it must be discussed," Spirit Bear said. "It changed me as you would expect. Any child who loses a parent is never the same. I lost both of mine at the same time, and one was the mightiest warrior in our band."

"I am sorry, *Woniya Mato*." Her eyes glittered with empathy for his pain.

"It is part of the reason I became so determined. *All events shape the person you become*," he answered. "I have come to terms with it, but the regret of the life we could have had will never diminish."

"*Tos*, my husband, it is true. I, too, changed when I lost my mother, so I know what you are saying. I cannot think about losing both parents at the same time."

Chief Spirit Bear

Chapter Seven
The Best and Worst Day: Nine Winters

Red Hawk had performed very well for the past winter. He was nearly at the top of his rank as warrior-in-training. Only grown men in the warrior community could best him consistently. His father was more than proud.

"*Cinks*, you have made me very honored! You are nine winters old and are a match for the best warriors-in-training."

"At least my friends are those matches you speak of," responded Red Hawk. "I do not think Sturdy Oak or Blue Jay would be happy if I bested them every match."

His father laughed, a bubbling of joy at his son's words.

"*Hiya*, they would not like it. They beat you one round, and then you best them. It won't be long, however, *Cinks*, that you will be the very top warrior-in-training. I would not be surprised if you are inducted into *Cante Tinza* with your rites into manhood."

Red Hawk's mouth was a perfect O-shape. "Really, Father?"

"You are the best I've ever seen, Red Hawk. I do not say that with father vision. I say that as war chief." His serious eyes looked down on his son with pride.

Red Hawk didn't know quite how to react. He was a humble boy, but he also was aware of his skill. It was the highest praise he'd ever received.

"It is a nice day. Let us celebrate with a meal away from home," Chief Takes Chances suggested. "I'll have your mother pack a nice dinner, and we will celebrate your prowess. How does that sound?"

"I would be honored, my father. Thank you." Red Hawk thought his head would lift him off the ground.

When his father went to prepare, Red Hawk sought out Straight Arrow. He shared with him what his father had said.

"That is wonderful, my friend," Straight Arrow said with a bright, slightly lopsided smile. "I always knew you were very gifted at winning! I would not want to compete against you at weaponry, stealth, or combat!"

"Nor would I want to get in a competition with you about medicine and spiritual incantations!" his friend exclaimed. "You have done as well in your field as I have in mine!"

Straight Arrow raised a brow. "Red Hawk, thank you, but you are good at everything!" he laughed.

"Everything I know about medicine, you have shared with me!" Red Hawk disputed.

"That may be, but you are just as apt of a student as am I! Besides, someday I may need help!" Straight Arrow's black eyes twinkled merrily.

"Ah, is that why you are teaching me, too?" Red Hawk laughed good-naturedly.

"*Tos*, of course! What better way to spend time with my spirit brother?"

"This is true!" Red Hawk stated.

"A band can never have too many healers," Straight Arrow said matter-of-factly.

"*Tos*," Red Hawk agreed, "I better go, my friend. Father wants to celebrate my progress with a family meal away from the village."

"That is nice," Straight Arrow said. "I am sure we will share a meal fire in one sun."

"Yes, we nearly always share meal fires. I am glad."

The boys clasped forearms and Red Hawk went to find his parents.

"*Cinks*, come with me. I have something for you," Chief Takes Chances said when he saw his son headed for their hut.

"What is it, Father?" Red Hawk asked, excitement lacing his words.

"It is a surprise. It is something you will need for your future as a *Cante Tinza* warrior."

Red Hawk was very curious. His eyes flashed in his face, and his body seemed to float with elation. They walked down toward the creek.

"Are we going to fish for the meat for our lunch?" Red Hawk asked. He could not stop the question from erupting from his lips.

"*Hiya*. Come just a little farther."

When they reached a grove of trees, Red Hawk saw a mare with a new foal. His father approached the bay, talking softly to her.

"Come," he repeated to his son.

Red Hawk tentatively walked forward. The new foal was not fearful of them, and he unsteadily approached them. The colt's bright, doe-like eyes were full of inquisitive wonder.

He snorted delicately and attempted a wobbly trot around them. The mare nickered reassuringly to her baby.

The foal's large, coppery spots gleamed in the sun, each an island surrounded by brilliant white. He had white stockings, black knees, and then the coppery color above that. His mane and tail were inky black with a strip of white where it lined his neck and at the top of his tail.

"What do you think of this colt?" Chief Takes Chances asked his son.

Almost as if on cue, the foal trotted back to Red Hawk and nudged his hand. The youth scratched the baby's neck.

"He is a very beautiful, Father. He is one of the prettiest I've ever seen!"

"He will make a wonderful war horse, *Cinks*. He has a strong build and wide chest. He is sturdy and will be a noteworthy animal. He is yours, and I want you to work with him daily."

"Thank you, Father! I am deeply honored!" Red Hawk felt as if his happy smile would split his face. *His father had just given him a war horse!*

"I also have a new filly I want to give you as well. She is to be used to start your own herd."

They walked to different spot not far away where another mare had just foaled. This mother was a deep liver chestnut with a white diamond and socks. Her new baby was a lighter color. The filly's tawny color flashed golden in the sun. She also had the dark legs, mane, and tail.

"These two babies should make outstanding horses when paired together. They will give you the jump on many horse owners. Your herd will be known across our seven nations," teased Chief Takes Chances.

Red Hawk was deeply moved by his father's generosity. In their culture, compliments were not freely given to the men of war. There was a delicate balance between not enough confidence and too much. A step in either direction could make a warrior fall, so compliments were hard-earned.

When Chief Takes Chances gave his son two exemplary horses to begin his own herd, Red Hawk understood the deeper, underlying pride his father was bestowing on him. This was his father's way of telling him just how proud of his achievements he was. Red Hawk's emotion welled up inside him. Before he could utter a response, he swallowed and took a breath. The love for his father soared to a higher level. All he'd ever wanted to do was make his father proud!

"Father, thank you," Red Hawk said. He cleared his throat and added, "I am greatly honored that you not only gave me a worthy war horse, but a mate for him as well!"

"I am very proud of your progress, Red Hawk. You already are a force to be reckoned with. The council knew what they were doing when they referred you for warrior training at eight winters. I couldn't be prouder." His father laid a hand on his shoulder.

"I will take care of these foals and work with them daily, Father. I am humbled by your gifts. Thank you." He looked up at his stoic parent.

"Good. Now let us go find your mother and see if she is ready to go. I am growing hungry."

"Are you ready to go, *Cinks*?" Bubbling Brook asked as she put the last food items in her basket. Her long black hair was a silky curtain that flowed with her movements.

"*Tos*, Mother. I am excited!" It was hard for Red Hawk not to bounce like a young boy with his exhilarating day. It had been wonderful so far, and it was only getting better.

"It has been a long time since we've been able to eat away from our tipi," she agreed. A slight dimple showed with her pleasure. "It is finally nice enough weather that we can enjoy ourselves!"

"Bring your arrows, *Cinks*," his father instructed. "We will catch fresh meat to eat rather than pack dried protein."

"*Tos*, I would be honored to help you gather meat!"

Bubbling Brook smiled with love. She enjoyed seeing her husband and their child interact. She, also, was looking forward for their meal. She had some exciting news to share herself.

"Maybe I can show you the horses Father gave me today," Red Hawk said excitedly. "Mother, they are very beautiful!"

"We are proud of you, Red Hawk! We are glad you like the gifts. If the horses are near, we will go with you to see them."

They left the house walking as one happy family. Chief Takes Chances held hands with his wife. Their son skipped ahead. When they got to the meadow, the males drew out their bows. Before long, a large rabbit was cooking on a spit over a fire.

"That was quite a shot, *Cinks*. Where did you learn to shoot like that?" his father teased him.

"*You* taught me, Father," Red Hawk said with a smile. "You just let me make the kill."

"You actually got to the draw faster than I," Takes Chances stated drily. His eyes twinkled happily. "I am glad I do not have to pit myself against you."

Red Hawk laughed. It was understood that his father was teasing him, but there was a little truth behind Takes Chance's words.

Takes Chances took the sizzling meat from the fire and cut it for his wife. Bubbling Brook was preparing the plates and cups while Red Hawk spread the woven blanket on the ground to cushion their bottoms. It acted as a buffer between them and the ground. It would keep them clean and shield them from the colder temperatures that still radiated up from the earth.

Bubbling Brook mixed greens together with a sort of dressing she'd made at home. It tasted of wild strawberries tinged with apple cider. She scooped the greens, freshly roasted rabbit, and pones of new bread onto each plate. Then she added a dollop of a sweet spread she'd made from honey and the rehydrated strawberries.

Red Hawk bit into the hot meat, and a burst of savory steam rose into the air as his teeth ripped off a chunk. The rabbit was slightly crisped on the outside, but tender and juicy in. A trace of warm grease trailed down his chin as he chewed.

"Mother, you cooked the rabbit to perfection!" he complimented.

"This is delicious!" agreed Takes Chances. "And so are the greens."

Before his mother could reply, Red Hawk exclaimed, "Father, taste the spread with the bread! It is out of this world!"

Bubbling Brook said, "Thank you, men of my life. A woman cannot have a higher compliment than those from her family."

"It is well-deserved, *wastelaka*," Takes Chances said.

Half way through the meal, Bubbling Brook smiled and said, "I have something I want to share with you this sun." She placed her plate on the blanket and smiled brightly.

Both of her men stopped eating to give her their full attention.

Bubbling Brook exclaimed, "Red Hawk is finally going to be a big brother!"

Takes Chances rocketed to his feet and swung her in a circle. "How long have you known, my wife?" He laughed deeply with unbridled joy. "And you're just now telling me?"

"I really only knew for sure this sun. I've suspected for about a week, but it is clear now. I wanted to tell you both on our special outing."

Red Hawk sat in stunned joy. *He was going to be a big brother? He couldn't believe it!* His chest filled with happiness as he imagined the future.

"Mother, I am so happy!" he said. "I will have so much to teach him!"

"Or her," agreed Bubbling Brook. Her face softened with the idea.

Red Hawk stopped to think about this new impression. *He might have a baby sister!* That opened up another whole realm of possibilities. He would have to watch over her and protect her from others. If it were a male child, he would have to help train him to fight and use weaponry. Both prospects appealed to him.

Takes Chances was jubilant. His features were dreamy and bright with joy. He kept hugging his wife tightly and running his hand tenderly down her glorious hair. Finally, the couple sat happily on the blanket.

After some time passed, Bubbling Brook collected the dirty dishes. Her husband helped. It was like he was floating on air. Red Hawk smiled. He'd never seen his father act so. He began to fold the blanket back, but his father stopped him.

"If you don't mind, *Cinks*, I will have a few moments of privacy with your mother."

Red Hawk grinned. Just then, he spied a highly unusual white fox.

"Okay, Father! I see a white fox. I will kill it for you, Mother!"

Quicker than a flash, Red Hawk was off.

A few hours later, a beautiful pelt in hand, Red Hawk appeared at Gentle Rabbit's entrance flap.

"*Hau*, Gentle Rabbit!" he called.

"What is it, Red Hawk?" she said, emerging from within. It was just after their rest time.

"Look! I killed this rare fox for my mother! Would you work your magic upon its skin?"

Gentle Rabbit took the pelt from him. She turned it over reverently in her hand and made a few exclamations to the rarity of the find.

"*Tos*! I would be happy to make this into a special gift!" she replied. "It is rare and magical."

"Thank you, my soul mother," he said with joy.

"By the way, Red Hawk, where is your mother?" Gentle Rabbit's brows raised with her question.

"They have not yet returned?" he asked, surprised.

"*Hiya*. I need her opinion on something."

"We ate a meal away from the village," Red Hawk replied. Then he added excitedly, "Did she tell you her news? Father was so thrilled that he wanted some time with her alone."

Gentle Rabbit's pretty face broke in a grin. "She did not tell me, but I live with *two* shamans," she said happily.

"I cannot believe it! I'm going to be a big brother!" Red Hawk said, elation bubbling through his normally calm exterior.

"You finally know?" asked Straight Arrow, coming from the tipi.

"And you did not tell me?" Red Hawk asked, gritting his teeth in play, feigning anger.

Straight Arrow laughed and held up his hands. "I would have, my brother, but it was not my place to tell you such big news."

"I wish they would come back. It's too exciting! I must look at this as warrior training," Red Hawk said. "I must calm my emotions and make myself wait patiently."

The boys busied themselves with games for a piece of time. Finally, Wind Walker approached.

"Red Hawk, where is your father?" he asked. The shaman's brow furrowed slightly.

Red Hawk told the story about their lunch, the request to be alone, the white fox, and his return to the village.

"They should have been back by now, I would think," said Wind Walker thoughtfully. He tried, unsuccessfully, to keep the trace of concern from his voice. "I think I will go and look for them."

"Do you care if I come along?" Red Hawk asked.

"*Hiya.* You may come as well, my son. I do not have a good feeling about this. Take some weapons just in case. I will ask a few other men to join us."

Red Hawk's brows knitted. It was not a good sign for the spiritual guide to have a premonition. "What do you believe is amiss?" he asked tentatively.

"Let us not waste time talking," Wind Walker said. "I hope my feeling is unfounded. If it is not, we need to make haste."

Quickly, Chief Tracking Dog and a handful of *Cante Tinza* warriors were perched atop of war horses. Two other horses were brought forth for the teens. As soon as everyone was mounted, the horses left at a gallop. Gentle Rabbit stood in the dust, wringing her hands.

Red Hawk led the posse, for he knew of his parents' exact location. When they thundered onto the site, a cold shudder racked the young warrior's body. He flew from his horse and charged toward the crumpled blanket left on the spring ground. The others were on his heels.

The dishes were left in a scattered disarray. Immediately, Red Hawk knew his mother would never do that. In fact, he'd watched her collect them and make a neat pile before he'd left.

"There are tracks left here," the hunting chief called. "There was a struggle."

The warriors fanned out, on high alert. When they paused to look toward their war chief's son, they saw a young boy holding up a blanket. His face was frozen in anguish. From his horrified expression, the warriors' eyes trailed to the blanket. Splashed boldly across the surface, a deep crimson stain was evidenced. It had soaked into the fabric, marring the simple beauty of the piece.

Red Hawk couldn't think; he couldn't breathe. A glacial numbness was spreading across his body. His hands were frozen into skeletal bird claws, clutched on the last remnants of his parents' life.

It was like Red Hawk was watching the scene from a remote location, from somewhere outside of himself. He viewed his body crumple to his knees, clasping the bloody blanket to his chest. Someone cried out. It was a horrible, wrenching sound; it was a keening that reached into his very soul. The wailing went on and on. Suddenly caught in a vacuum that pulled him back into his body, Red Hawk realized that he was the one screaming.

Straight Arrow lay a sympathetic and mourning hand upon his hearth brother's shoulder and turned him. Red Hawk grabbed his friend and hugged him tightly. It was a few moments before he could collect his wits and calm himself.

The other warriors searched the vicinity, weapons ready. However, it was too late. All that remained of his parents were the stained blanket, scattered dishes, and the smashed basket. The scuffed ground showed the battle that had occurred, but there were no bodies. Red Hawk's beloved guardians had disappeared, and all he had left were their memories.

Chapter Eight
Grief

"Oh, *Woniya Mato*! That story is even more horrible than I had imagined!" cried Kaitlin. "Your mother was *pregnant*!"

Kaitlin's face crumpled. Tears began to leak out of her eyes at his terrible losses. She could not imagine losing her baby. She also could not face it if their child was abandoned, unintentionally, by them.

Spirit Bear hugged her tightly to him and stroked her hair. "Shhh, *wastelaka*," he soothed. "It was a very difficult time in my life, but I have come to terms with my grief."

"How, my husband? How can a child the age of nine come to terms with it?" she cried.

"I had no other choice," he said simply. "I repressed my anguish for many years, and I took it out on my opponents."

Kaitlin took a deep breath and wiped her eyes. She asked, "During your training?"

He nodded, a flicker of regret in his eyes. "I am surprised I still have friends. I was ruthless."

"Um, you still are, *wastelaka*," she said, offering a shaky smile. "I am sure your friends understand. I am sure they are thankful to call you *kola* rather than *toka*."

He nodded. "There was only one other time in my life where I feared as much as I did that sun."

"What sun is that, my husband?" Kaitlin held her breath. She didn't know if she could hear another heart-rending story just yet.

Spirit Bear smiled gently when he said, "When Sly Coyote stole you from my side."

Kaitlin leaned her head against him. She sighed softly into his strength. Briefly she recalled the Crow-Yankton man. He'd come to her one evening before her wedding celebration and told her that her betrothed had been attacked by the Crow, their enemy, and he might not make it through the night. Kaitlin had been in a panic and had jumped on the horse he'd so generously brought. The man had tricked her to kidnap her and use her as bait to try to kill their greatest foe, Chief Spirit Bear. She forced Sly Coyote from her mind and returned to the story of her husband's past.

"You went to live with Wind Walker and Gentle Rabbit?" she prompted gently.

"*Tos*. Gentle Rabbit has always been a mother figure to me. She and Wind Walker welcomed me with open arms into their home."

"Did it help you with your healing path? You lived with two spiritual advisors," Kaitlin explained her reasoning.

"Their love and acceptance helped more than anything, but it was a rough time for me. It was a period I had to work through my emotions on my own. Having their care was wonderful and did help me progress through my rage faster." Spirit Bear paused and then added, "I am thankful for their support."

"How many years were you angry?"

"Many. I hid it well. I still had fun with my friends, but my rage didn't evaporate until I killed Night Hawk."

"Sly Coyote's father?" Kaitlin held her breath as she waited for his answer.

"*Tos, Mazaska Zi Ista*. Sly Coyote's father was my first warrior kill. Actually, I didn't become a recognized warrior until after that event," Spirit Bear explained. "The *Cante Tinza* suspected my parents were slain and taken by the Crow, so my fury knew no bounds when it came to them. My coup released all that emotion. I realized I killed a boy's father in front of him, and nothing evaporates anger faster than guilt.

"In fact, the *Cante Tinza* suspected it was the very man's life I took who was responsible for my parents' demise. I would have killed him all over again, only not in front of his son."

"How old were you at the time?" she asked.

"Twelve winters."

"The age of most boys as they enter into warrior training."

"For many, *tos*."

There wasn't anything Kaitlin could say to assuage his guilt or lessen the pain of the past, so she remained quiet. She reached out to touch his smooth skin. She absently traced the veins twisting under his skin as she listened to his current revelation unfold in his rise to power.

Chief Spirit Bear

Chapter Nine
First Coup: Twelve Winters

"Red Hawk, come with us!" Yellow Jacket invited. "We will be running some warrior training drills. You are better than most of us, so will you join our group?" He smiled, happy to have one-up on the other party.

"*Tos*," Black Snake agreed. "You are a natural leader, also. We would like to hear your strategies during a mock-attack. If we break into two parties for 'warring' purposes, we want you to lead our group."

Red Hawk laughed, delight etched across his features. It was a distinct compliment to be accepted by those already in warrior status. "I am honored you asked. *Tos*, I will come."

"Bring both real and practice weaponry," Spotted Horse said. "We also plan to hunt."

Red Hawk nodded then turned to prepare. Not long after, he was astride his muscular war horse, for the large steed needed the practice raid as well.

Red Hawk had taken a lot of time and pride on the training of this horse. It was the last gift from his father, and the stallion had special meaning. Chief Takes Chances had been right. *Runs with the Wind* was an example of what a war horse should be. He was large and powerful, but he was quick, intelligent, and graceful as well. *Runs with the Wind* fought alongside him. He would bite, kick, and paw any person he fought.

"Where are we setting up our mock battle?" Red Hawk asked Yellow Jacket.

"Just within our band's territory."

"Crow boundary side?" Red Hawk asked with a smirk.

"*Tos.*"

"Can we invite them to play?" he asked only half teasing. Red Hawk checked the feather guides on his arrow shafts in a show of being ready to kill.

"*Hiya*, my friend. Save your combat for your warrior moons," Yellow Jacket laughed. Everyone in the Bear Claw Clan knew Red Hawk's feelings about the Crow.

"There will be twenty of us; you are with our group, and the other group is meeting elsewhere to strategize," Yellow Jacket informed.

"Okay."

"By the way, you are planner for our team," Yellow Jacket added with a wide smile.

"What?" Red Hawk asked in surprise. Although they had mentioned his leadership during the invite, he didn't think they really wanted him to initiate the ploys.

"The other group said it wasn't fair that our group got you!" Spotted Horse said with a snort. "I agree! Since you haven't led a raid before, they denoted you. They erroneously think because you've never strategized one, it could give them a tiny advantage. It's the only way they'd let us have you without a fight."

Black Snake said, "They don't *really* believe that. They just did not want to lose face knowing you were on our team, so we agreed." He laughed and the others joined in.

Red Hawk was honored they thought so highly of him. In a way, it made him nervous. *They had faith in him! What if his strategy didn't work? Would he lose power as a son of a war chief?* He only wished to honor his late father.

Once the group had arrived at their destination, Red Hawk had them gather round. He'd had time to think of a war strategy on their ride there. His eyes glowed and his gestures were animated as he relayed his plan.

"You have the *best* ideas!" Yellow Jacket cried in glee. "You should be war chief! There is no way they will claim coup on us with this plan!"

"I hope you are right," said Red Hawk. He tried to appear confident, but it was his first time planning a raid.

"We cannot lose with your strategy," Black Snake approved. "Come. We move!"

Each band of Oglala warriors silently crept toward the other. Even the horses were stealthy. Their war paint camouflage helped them blend into the scenery.

All at once, the Oglala came upon an interesting sight. Red Hawk's eyes grew wide when he saw what was in front of him. Five Crow warriors and a young boy were on their lands!

Instantly, his vision went red. Adrenaline surged through his body and vitalized him to another plane. Things appeared to be in slow motion; Red Hawk heard every noise, felt every vibration. He even believed he could hear their thoughts.

The twelve-year old felt like a grown man; he was invincible. He felt his father's spirit hovering above him, guiding him. He signaled for his band to stop and surround the enemy. Immediately upon his gesture, they obeyed.

Suddenly one of the Crow horses made a noise, indicating that they'd been discovered. A change came over their foes. They'd been intently stalking up until this point, but it hadn't been the type of poise a man of war would use on another with the intent of ambush. It was more of what the bands did while hunting. After the horse's warning, that swiftly changed. Immediately on high alert, bows went up and their watchful eyes scanned the shrubbery for a hint of ill intent.

Red Hawk gave the sign. He led the crusade against the Crow. He popped up suddenly and fired his bow with terrible war cry. His arrow struck the black heart of the one in the lead. The other men who followed wore shocked expressions of disbelief. Their reactions were delayed only by seconds, but it was enough. Quickly following Red Hawk's missile, other arrows were instantly unleashed. The remaining men in the party could not avoid the daggers of death. All that were left in a matter of moments were rider-less horses and a young boy who not too much younger that Red Hawk himself.

The boy gripped his horse in terror, and the animal was shying and rearing away from the smell of death. Black Snake came up to the mare and calmed it. Then he grabbed the boy and lowered him to the ground.

"Red Hawk! You just won your first battle as war leader!" Yellow Jacket said with a huge grin. "You earned your first true coups. Not only did you direct us, you made first kill. We are honored to follow one such as you!"

Spotted Horse said, "You also claim the belongings of the man you killed. His horse is yours. You can choose the boy's horse as well."

Red Hawk nodded once. His expression was unreadable as he watched the Crow youth. The boy ran to his father's side and wailed. He crouched in agony, touching his father's dead form. He rocked back and forth, oblivious to the enemy warriors surrounding him.

Red Hawk was transported back in time to when he had experienced the same sense of loss; the major difference being he did not witness his father's death. Red Hawk never got the closure of seeing his father's body being lifted on a scaffold with his death rites chanted, but he also did not have to see his loved one's life ebb away before his eyes.

When the boy no longer cried, he just crouched before his father's body, rocking back and forth. Red Hawk approached him.

"Come, we will take you back to our village."

"*Hiya!*" he cried hotly.

"He speaks Lakota at his age?" Black Snake asked in surprise.

All the men stared at him. It was not uncommon for them to know Crow or for the other tribe to speak Lakota, but usually it was with much older men.

The boy looked up at them, his black eyes blades of obsidian.

"Come," Red Hawk repeated.

The dagger eyes narrowed in hate as they sought him out.

"You killed my father!" he screamed.

Red Hawk swallowed. He felt terrible that the boy's father had to die in front of him. Guilt surged like bile in his throat. It tampered his anger that he'd nursed for years against the Crow.

"You were in our territory," Red Hawk replied after a few moments. "I am sorry for your loss and that you had to witness that, but the last time your people were on our lands, *my* father died."

"We were only hunting!" the boy cried, "We did not realize we were on your lands!"

"If you had seen us first, I am sure the result would have been similar," Red Hawk declared.

The boy fell silent, and then he began to tremble. He was becoming aware of his predicament after his anguish had eased a little. He was surrounded by the enemy, and they had just killed all in his party.

Finally, he asked, "Why did you spare me?"

"You are not yet a warrior," Red Hawk said.

Yellow Jacket added, "We do not kill children. How old are you?"

"I am eight winters." The boy's teeth were starting to chatter.

"What is your name?" Black Snake asked.

"Jumping Fox."

"How do you know Lakota?" Red Hawk pressed.

"My mother was Yankton." The words were soft, barely audible.

Again, his words had stunned the warriors. Just then, the second party of Bear Claw Clan erupted onto the scene. It took a few moments for them to absorb what had happened.

"Come, Jumping Fox. We return to our village," Yellow Jacket said. "We will take you to the Yankton. First, we must alert the chiefs to the new development."

Chapter Ten
Understanding

"Woniya Mato," Kaitlin said, "that is quite a tale of your first coup."

She continued to stroke his skin in compassion. He watched her golden hand on his bronzed arm. His eyes were thoughtful, reflective.

She searched for more words, but at the moment they were evasive. The blonde had always thought that warriors were cold-hearted machines when they were in their war mode, but now she realized what a traumatic event it truly was for them.

Not only had Spirit Bear lost his own father, but her husband had had to relive it when he took the guilty man's life. His regret was shadowed by the knowledge that the young Sly Coyote had watched his father die by his hands.

Did Spirit Bear feel responsible for how the boy had turned out? Did he blame himself for Sly Coyote's revenge and ultimately, her capture? Did it have any bearing on the havoc the Oglala had wrecked on the Crow that fateful day? Kaitlin wasn't sure how much she should press him.

"That sun, so long ago, released all the hate from my heart. It made a better man of me," he finally said.

"Did you realize that Sly Coyote was that same boy, Jumping Fox, when we met him at our wedding gathering?" Kaitlin asked.

"Other things were on my mind, *wastelaka*. *Hiya*, I did not recognize him," Spirit Bear admitted. "It was a huge loss of power which is why he was able to lure you from beneath my very nose. When a warrior becomes lax, that is when things happen."

"I am sure, my husband, that you were not negligent. You believed all to come our pre-wedding ceremony to be *kolas*. One would not think you'd have to be on high alert among friends," she tried to reassure.

"I am head war chief," Spirit Bear disagreed. "A war chief is never careless. Otherwise, he endangers himself and his entire band, and lives are lost when he is not on alert."

Kaitlin could not argue. She was not a war chief; nor was she responsible for all the lives in their village.

Instead, she said, "*Woniya Mato*, is every kill you must make so difficult for you?"

"Every life I take is a serious matter," he confirmed solemnly. "Each man killed is a loved one. He leaves a wife, mother, child, or sibling behind to mourn for him. However, that first kill was the one that affected me the deepest."

"*Tos*, I understand," she soothed. "Do you forgive yourself?"

"Finally, I do. I shall always have regret over what happened with Sly Coyote. He made his own decisions, but I feel a little responsible that he was not able to transition to his life in the Yankton village more thoroughly."

They lay a little longer reassuring each other by touch in the warm glow of the fire. The soft popping soothed them, and Kaitlin watched the shadows dance on the walls of their home. Before she knew it, she had drifted off to sleep.

Upon waking, Kaitlin felt at peace. Her husband's arm was draped over her, a band of security. She snuggled up closer to her husband and allowed her satisfaction and love for him to wash over her. She thanked the Great Spirit for her life and her heart sang with pride for her husband. He was even more perfect than she'd ever realized, and she'd always felt him to be perfect for her.

Finally, she grew uncomfortable. She rolled over and said, "I need to take a trip to the area of privacy, my husband. Will you walk that direction with me?"

"*Tos, wastelaka.*" He smiled tenderly at her and hugged her before rising.

"I will refill our *mniapahta* while we are near the creek," she said. "Then I will start our lunch meal."

The handsome chief nodded agreement. The couple got up and dressed. Spirit Bear added a few sticks to the fire. Then he grabbed his bow and arrows as they exited their tipi.

"I will get a fish if I can while you take care of your business," he said.

Kaitlin nodded. She felt it was a good idea after he had shared so deeply. By being active, her husband would relieve a bit of the increasing stress from reliving past events.

When she stooped at the stream to fill water into the bags, he held up two flipping silvery fish. Kaitlin smiled in pleasure at his catch.

"Come, let us return," Spirit Bear said with a vibrant smile. "The wind is picking up, and another round of rain is blowing in. I will clean these fish if you will make a soup with them."

"I would be happy to, my husband," she responded with a returned smile.

After they ate, Kaitlin said, "Do you need a break from your story, my husband?"
"*Hiya, wastelaka*. I will tell you more if you wish."
"Would you tell me about your manhood ceremony?"
"*Tos*, but first I will tell you about my vision quest."

Chapter Eleven
Spirit Bear: Twelve Winters

Within a few days of Red Hawk's first coup, Chief Storm Cloud approached him.

"Red Hawk, I would like to hold a ceremony in a few suns," he began.

Red Hawk nodded. His features were more on the solemn side lately.

"I want to celebrate your first coup. You will be honored and welcomed into manhood. You also will be adopted into the *Cante Tinza*," he revealed with huge grin.

Red Hawk was happy about that, but he was still struggling with the blood on his hands. The chief noticed the boy's reaction; it wasn't quite what he'd expected.

"Son, your first war kill is the hardest. Yours was even more so," Chief Storm Cloud said. "It dug up all your feelings for the loss of your father. This is normal. Even if you feel… guilty."

"Really?" he managed past the threatening lump in his throat. With effort, he swallowed.

"*Tos.* You lost your father who would normally counsel you to help you through the feelings of your first kill. What you need to do is go on a vision quest. This will help you heal from your sadness over having to take a life. We all must do this, and it will help."

"*Tos*, Chief Storm Cloud."

The sympathetic man's face reflected his compassion for Red Hawk's youthful pain. He added, "And it will reveal your adult name to you. It will bring you power. Do not be ashamed of the man you are. You are pride-worthy. Go on your quest and heal, my son. Upon your return, we celebrate!"

"I need to see Wandering Elk, first, right?" Red Hawk asked.

"*Tos*. He will purify you for your mission. Take a filled pipe with you. You will also need to take extra to smoke while on your quest."

Red Hawk nodded. He went to gather what he'd need from the tipi. For the first time since his coup, he had a slight spring in his step. He'd received the confirmation he didn't know he needed. *It was normal for a man to feel regret for a coup!*

Wind Walker appeared at the tipi's entrance flap just as he was leaving the dwelling. The kind, fatherly figure took in the items Red Hawk held at a glance.

"Is it time for a vision quest, my son?" he asked with a prideful nod. "You are a man now."

"Is it difficult, Hearth Father?" he responded.

"It depends on if the spirits are willing. For some, it is difficult, and some do not experience a vision on their first attempt. You, my son, will not have any trouble. Your spiritual guides are strong."

"*Tos*. Thank you. Will you tell Gentle Rabbit and Straight Arrow?"

"*Tos*, I am honored to relay your reasons for being gone."

"*Hau*, Wandering Elk?" Red Hawk called at his entrance flap.

"*Hau*. Come in, Red Hawk."

The young man ducked inside. The elder was sitting on a woven mat of natural colors.

"You come to begin a spirit quest?" Wandering Elk asked rhetorically. He stood without waiting for an answer. "Let us go to the lodge for a cleanse."

"*Tos*, Wandering Elk."

The tipi was already hot inside. The fire roared in the pit, and by now, incense thickly perfumed the air. It clung in pockets of heat.

"Storm Cloud informed me that you'd be seeking me today, so he equipped the lodge for our use."

Red Hawk's eyes widened momentarily with surprise.

"Come, we prepare. Storm Cloud will be our helper. We must cleanse."

Red Hawk hadn't been involved in an *Inipi* Ceremony, or true cleansing rite, before. He wasn't sure what to expect.

Almost as if reading his thoughts, Wandering Elk stated, "First you need to strip. Take a seat by the fire. We sweat out our impurities. When Storm Cloud adds to the fire, he will also add more incense, and we will smoke. Then we meditate until the process begins again."

Red Hawk nodded understanding.

At that time, Storm Cloud reentered the tipi with an arm full of wood. He piled more onto the fire, and then he stripped and sat with them.

Wandering Elk said, "Red Hawk, I will explain the process in further detail to you. You are very young to go on a vision quest, but yet you are a man. If the spirits find you worthy of man status, your guide will reveal your name to you."

"I understand," said Red Hawk.

"Do you have a place chosen to commune with the Great Spirit and all life?" Wandering Elk's eyes studied his face.

"Tos," he replied seriously with a nod.

"Tell me of your sacred ground. I will send Wind Walker there to purify the location. Once you have been cleansed, you will go there. Take incense and your pipe to smoke, but nothing else. You may not eat or drink until your vision seeking is over."

"I understand, *Wicasa Wakan*, Holy One."

"This quest can occur the first day, Red Hawk, but often it does not. It can take three to four days. If your spirit helper has not visited you by the third day, you must return. You are the youngest in our band to ever attempt this, and it can be dangerous. If your spirit guide does not come to you in three days, you are not yet ready."

Red Hawk nodded his understanding.

"Do not worry about keeping track of days. Wind Walker will monitor you and keep you safe. He will take turns with his son. They both have deep knowledge of spirits and understand the gravity of your purpose. They will not interrupt or speak with you."

"*Tos*. Thank you, Wandering Elk and Chief Storm Cloud."

"Now we smoke."

Red Hawk had smoked a pipe before, but not for any period of time. As he breathed in the smoke, the heavy perfume, and the heated air, his head began to swim. The lodge was so hot. Already sweat was trickling down his head and dripping off his nose.

It was a mindset. He had to ignore his physical discomfort and internalize. He had to wipe every thought from his awareness. Once his concentration was free from activity, the spirits would visit, or he would call on their world.

Red Hawk sat straight and tall, but suddenly, he felt a mild pop in his crown. His head dropped to his chest, and he was free. It was a thoughtless, mindless feeling. He floated above himself and watched in a disinterested way. When he looked down and saw them seated around the blaze, it was merely as an observation. After a few moments, he felt himself rise further, and then a sense of deep relaxation came over his body.

When he awoke later, both men in the hut were watching him closely.

"You experienced immediately what takes us hours," Chief Storm Cloud said. "You are ready to go on your quest."

Red Hawk felt drugged, but he nodded once. His body was very heavy, and he still felt as if he were dreaming. In a disjointed way, he rose and collected his pipe and tobacco. He donned his clothes and without talking, Wind Walker and Straight Arrow accompanied him to his chosen location.

Once there, Red Hawk assumed an Indian style with his backbone ramrod straight. He was seated on a rock ledge looking down upon his village. His sweat had dried, and he felt a peaceful mindfulness. Physical distractions tried to interrupt; his body tried to divert his attention with a craving for water. Pushing back the cry for liquid, Red Hawk smoked his pipe and once more turned his focus internally.

On the second day of his fast, Red Hawk's spiritual guide paid him a visit. The late afternoon sun was warm on his body, and a slight breeze kissed his skin. Red Hawk sat quietly with his eyes closed.

A vibration began to thrum through the young warrior's body, and in a flash of brilliant light, a halo of purity cut through the hazy fog of his brain. Although his eyes weren't open, the young man could see. The light was so pure and so bright, it was nearly impossible to comprehend.

The essence began to pulse; it shrunk and expanded with his heartbeats. It stretched and twisted elegantly until an enormous bear was before him. It didn't stand, nor did it float; it just was. The animal's eyes were the color of crystalized topaz. When it opened its mouth, the bear did not roar but spoke to him gently. The voice was the intonation of his father's.

"Red Hawk? Visit with me."

"Father?" Red Hawk asked quietly.

The bear answered, "I am all that is. I am *Wakantanka*. I am your father. I am also your future."

Red Hawk was focused on the one response for a moment. "Father? Father, I miss you so much!"

"And I, you, *Cinks*."

Those words brought tears to his son's eyes.

"You are a man, now, *Cinks*," the bear said softly. "Men do not cry."

"What do you do to handle these floods of emotion, Father? I miss you and Mother so much! I also feel guilty for my anger! I killed a boy's father in front of him."

The brilliant animal replied, "You must learn to let some of your emotions go. Channel it into raw power. Let go of your guilt and realize that you saved people in your village. Your heart knew to slay the Crow before you were targeted. That warrior would not have thought twice about killing you despite your age."

Red Hawk was considering the bear's words.

The spiritual beast continued, "You acted as a warrior would, as a war chief. That is your destiny, *Cinks*. You will become the mightiest fighter of your time. You have been chosen and marked by *Wakantanka*."

The boy's eyes grew until they were the size of eggs. He could think of no response.

"Your reign will begin after you defeat a bear in hand combat."

"I must fight a bear?" he asked in awe.

"You *are* a bear in human form, and the essence of the bear is in you. You must connect the two and harness the power. First, your animal opponent must mark you. Forever after, you will be able to call on the wise one's spirit when you are in need, and he will come."

"Thank you, Father."

"Remember, I am all that is. I am here if you know where to look. Always thank *Wakantanka*, and I will reward you, and always stay humble."

"Yes, Father."

"I must go. Take my message to Wandering Elk. He will guide you."

"Father, will I see you again?" Red Hawk asked. He wanted to hear more. He called, "How is Mother?"

But the bear was gone.

As promised, the ceremony was within a handful of days after Red Hawk's quest. There was excitement buzzing around the community. It was said that the prowess of the young warrior was going to be recognized.

The celebration began as all others did. First, the new women were recognized followed by the men. There was dancing, music, and other forms of entertainment. This festivity was more entailed than the one prior, however. There was a war event and real coups to announce!

Finally, there were only three boys left to become men. Sturdy Oak, one of Red Hawk's closest friends, was called to the front first.

Chief Storm Cloud began, "Sturdy Oak, we are very proud of your accomplishments. You are a remarkable warrior, but even above that, you are a gifted hunter."

Chief Hunting Dog added, "It was a difficult decision for the council to make, but we have decided to make you a warrior even though it is evident you enjoy the thrill of the hunt. Your prowess is too great for mere woodsman status; however, we would like to see you lead some of our larger hunting expeditions."

"I am honored, my chiefs!" said Sturdy Oak beaming, "Thank you for my recognition!"

"Now we will ask you to reveal your name given during your vision quest," Chief Storm Cloud said.

"My totem is a wolf, and my name is to be Lone Wolf."

The chiefs smiled and repeated it back. Then the throng did the same and then lent their voices to show support.

Wandering Elk placed an eloquently decorated wolf *wanapin* over his head. It contained feather adornments, and the leather thong holding the medallion contained alternating gray and gold stones.

"Please stay near the stage," Chief Tracking Dog said with a grin.

"Blue Jay, please step forward," Chief Storm Cloud directed.

A young man, tall and athletic looking, stepped forward. He was one of Red Hawk's closest friends. He was dressed in finely fringed leather garments.

"Has your totem revealed himself to you?" asked Wandering Elk.

"Tos. My totem is the warrior of the skies, the eagle."

"And your name?" the shaman asked.

"Sky Warrior."

The name was repeated, and he was given a carved eagle *wanapin*. Chalcedony and bone beads helped to decorate the necklace along with eagle feathers.

"You will be joining warrior ranks!" Chief Storm Cloud announced. The crowd loudly cheered their support. Sky Warrior walked to stand by Lone Wolf.

"Red Hawk, please join us!"

The gathering was excited, and they waited expectantly.

"You are the youngest man to ever be named a warrior!" revealed Chief Storm Cloud.

"And the youngest to go on a vision quest," added Wandering Elk.

The mass of Oglala waited on bated breath.

"Did your totem reveal himself to you?" The shaman knew that he had but always asked for dramatic effect.

"*Tos*. My spirit guide is the bear."

The crowd was deafening. The bear was the mightiest totem to mark a warrior; it was highly esteemed as a spirit guide. Because the band was named after the mighty animal, a warrior had a lot of pressure to live up to the name.

When the noise level lowered, Wandering Elk said, "What is your warrior's name, Red Hawk?"

"Spirit Bear."

The support from the crowd surged in decibels again. After a time, Wandering Elk was able to speak.

"Spirit Bear, what did your totem reveal to you?"

"He said I would be a mighty warrior but I would need to fight a bear so that we could mark each other."

The crowd gasped and fell silent.

Chief Tracking Dog asked, "You must fight a bear in hand combat?"

"*Tos*. He said I must fight at least one. My totem guide said once I defeated the bear, I could always call upon his power."

The crowd was silent now, pride and disbelief marking their level of attention.

"This *wanapin* I am placing on your neck symbolizes your name, but as you know, you may not wear bear claws or teeth until the bear honors you with them."

"Tos." Spirit Bear was humble. He looked down at the like replica of a grizzly in movement. The wood carving was detailed. He could see the bear's hair on his coat, his nostrils, and even the pupils in his eyes. His trade-marked feathers, those of the red-tailed hawk, decorated the *wanapin* along with red jasper stone and onyx beads.

"Thank you, my chiefs! I will wear this with honor!" he cried.

"As you know," Chief Storm Cloud began facing the people, "We lost our war chief three years ago." He raised his hands to the heavens, palms up. Then his dark eyes dropped back to the crowd. "Before Chief Takes Chances, his father, Chief Sleeping Bear, was war chief."

Wandering Elk took over, "We have not found an adequate replacement to fill the shoes of war chief. And now we know the reason."

Chief Storm Cloud said, "Spirit Bear is not yet ready to walk as war chief, but it has been revealed that he will be the strongest one that this band has seen yet!"

Spirit Bear's eyes widened and he swallowed hard. He knew what his guide had told him, but he did not know this part.

"We will share the responsibilities of war chief until our young warrior is ready to fill those shoes. It may take months, or it may take years, but we feel it is the will of *Wakantanka.*"

The response was surreal. The Oglala roared and then performed a stomping celebration around the ceremonial grounds.

Finally, the multitude began to calm. Chief Storm Cloud assumed the center of the clearing. He waited until there was no sound emanating from the crowd.

"My people, it is time to honor these three men with the highest of honors." Chief Storm Cloud exclaimed with a smile. "Would the new men Spirit Bear, Sky Warrior, and Lone Wolf please come forward? They will be joining the *Cante Tinze!*"

Wandering Elk walked forward with the rest of the Tribal Council to join the three proud men. The leading society took turns going into depth of why these fine men were being inducted into The *Cante Tinze*, or Brave Hearts. Only warriors with the highest statuses and the most earned coups who had years of displayed prowess and bravery could enter this elite society.

The crowd's wild cheering was thunderous.

Chief Takes Chances held his war knife high in the air. The afternoon sun glittered down the deadly blade. The throng quieted with expectation. Grasping the war weapon's edge with his left hand, the war chief slid the honed tip down his hand, slicing the meat open. The five other members of the Tribal Council did the same with the war chief's knife. Then they sliced the hands of each new inductee. Afterwards, the new members of the warrior society grasped the bloody hands of his leaders. The community's voices shouted with support and admiration.

"Lean forward to accept your *Cante Tinze wanapin* in honor," Chief Storm Cloud said loudly. Wandering Elk placed the totem around each of the three warriors' necks.

Chief Takes Chances said, "Spirit Bear, Lone Wolf, and Sky Warrior, protectors of the people of the Bear Claw Clan of the Oglala, members of the *Cante Tinze* Society, meet your people!"

All members of the elite warrior society gathered on the stage and welcomed the new members.

"Behold, the *Cante Tinza*!" Chief Storm Cloud cried.

The supreme men of war performed a very short dance and then walked around to outrageous support generated from the gathered people. Each member made a grand exit of showing off a physical skill. Of them, only Black Wolf, a leading warrior, remained. He did a singular war dance with his knife that ended with a terrifying war cry. Afterwards, all men left the clearing to outrageous applause and voice support.

Chief Spirit Bear

Chapter Twelve
The Bear Chooses

"You knew you would someday be war chief when you were twelve winters?" Kaitlin asked incredulously. "That seems so young for so much to have happened to you!"

"*Wakantanka* only tests those who are truly worthy," he replied simply.

"That may be so, but it just seems..." Kaitlin searched for a word, "unbelievable that you had so much on your shoulders at that age."

Kaitlin thought back to her early life. In the white man's world, children really did not have much responsibility. They were taught manners and how to act properly for their role in society, but they did not assume any tasks that were overly important. They would never have been asked to carry out a task that might cost them their lives or one of someone else.

Kaitlin's brows furrowed a tiny amount as she thought of the child she carried. In the past, she'd never have given a thought as to what a youth of twelve might be asked to do while in her society. It was a given then they'd be protected until they were at least sixteen. Never would she have considered that a twelve-year-old might be assuming a protective man role which could cost him his life! It was concerning to the blonde.

The attractive warrior shrugged. "It was an honor to be chosen," he said. "The Great Spirit begins to test the worthy earlier in life."

It was not an arrogant statement, but one he truly believed.

"*Woniya Mato*, my husband, I am so proud of you. You have gone through many trials and tribulations so young, and you still have a positive outlook. You did not allow life to harden your soul."

He smiled. His white teeth were a stark contrast against his bronze skin. "For the three years after my parents' death, I would not have agreed with you. But I learned peace and forgiveness through the guilt of my actions. I learned that revenge is not a satisfying way to assuage the pain of the past. However, it is necessary many times to guarantee peace for the future."

Kaitlin had been with the band long enough to see these words were true. She nodded in agreement. With her action, the fire reflected on her hair and sent blazing shimmers down its golden length.

Spirit Bear reached up to touch the soft vibrancy. He held a strand between his forefinger and thumb and watched as it tried to twist around his hand. Even with the small effort, his muscles bunched and rippled under his skin.

"It is amazing that you can capture the power of the sun with your body," the warrior said as he watched her hair sparkle in the light.

His wife laughed. "I do not have the power of the sun, my husband."

"You do," he insisted. "You have much power, *wastelaka*. More than you know."

Kaitlin didn't respond. *How did she have power?* she wondered. Yet, her husband was not the only one to tell her so. When she had visited the Crow band against her will, many there believed her to be powerful as well. Most had treated her with reverence.

Spirit Bear asked, "How do you think you became my wife?"

"Because I was lucky and found a bear claw?" she responded.

"*Hiya, wastelaka*. The Great Spirit knew our clan needed more than just a simple sign. He gave many. How many times did the She-Bear visit you?" His eyes twinkled merrily as he tried to make his point.

"Hum. Let's see. There was the time at the cabin when she ate my fish stew..."

"Which you walked away from without a scratch," he said with a grin.

"I was safe in the tree," she refuted. "She didn't pay me any attention."

"She knew you were there," he said pointedly, "and as I recall, she could have easily climbed those thick and sloping branches had she wanted." He paused then said, "Go on."

"Then she visited me that time I was at the Tipis Apart," she said thoughtfully. "But you were there to protect me."

"The Great Spirit wanted me to see that she sniffed you and approved! Mother bears are highly protective of their young, and she had her babies with her at that time. That is also when she left you the gift of her claw." Spirit Bear reached down to touch the *wanapin* she wore around her neck. "She honored you above warriors. Very few men are able to wear a *mato* gift, and they have to fight for it. Here you are, a mere *winyan*, and you wear a much-sought-after claw that was freely given."

Kaitlin shook her head. Yes, she'd been lucky on *several* occasions, but it was difficult for her to believe that it was a godly sign.

As if reading her mind, Spirit Bear said, "Things happen for a reason, *Mazaska Zi Ista*. There are no mistakes. It was not mere coincidence that you met the She-Bear so many times and was never harmed."

"But... the next time I met her, she ate my berries, and I was in another tree," she said uncertainly. "And the last time was when she killed Snake Strike for harming her cub."

"You and Brave Elk were within her reach, yet she took her babies and left. You were marked as being worthy of Oglala status and ultimately, as my wife."

"I am so thankful, too," she said deciding not to argue further. "I cannot stand to be a slave."

"*Wakantanka* knew, but I was slow to catch on," he said with a laugh, "so He had to make me see through my totem – the bear." His warm fingers trailed down the line of her collarbone. His hand circled around to the nape of her neck, and then he ran his fingers up into the mass of her honeyed tresses. Fisting her hair gently, he pulled her face to his and kissed her deeply.

"I love you, my wife. I am excited to bring our child into our home."

"Me, too, my husband. I cannot wait to be a family." She traced his strong jawline gently then leaned forward to nibble his full lips.

They kissed again, tongues dancing. When she pulled back, his eyes were gleaming. They studied each other with eyes of love. Outside their tipi, the wind snarled and growled. A few splatters of rain began.

"Will you tell me about your fight with the bear?" she asked after their heartbeats had begun to slow.

"*Tos*, but first I will tell you of the Sun Dance. It is something members of our tribe do to show our bravery and courage. Since I am telling you my tale in chronological order, I will begin with this first."

"The Sun Dance?" Kaitlin asked. "Why does a dance need bravery and courage? Because you do it in front of everyone at a young age?"

"*Hiya, Mazaska Zi Ista*. This is a very important and sacred event where many bands in our tribe unite. We meet so our fighters can earn coup in the time the Earth renews itself. It is not necessarily a dance as you think of it, but it is a way for warriors to show their daring. It is very dangerous, and can be fatal. We have many medicine men and holy men there to help heal the dancers afterwards."

"It is hard for me to imagine this," Kaitlin said. "It is spring now, my husband. Will the dance be performed soon?"

The blonde was curious and apprehensive about it now. It was a bit unnerving as she didn't like to watch dangerous events.

"*Tos*. Those who wish to participate will leave in a handful of suns. Our village is large, so only the chosen ones, their supporters, and our medicine and shaman will go."

"How old were you, *wastelaka*?"

"I was fifteen winters when I undertook the Sun Dance."

"*Tos*, I would like to know all about this rite!" Kaitlin said as she settled in next to him. She really was enjoying this day of relaxation, warmth, and learning more about him. It helped her understand more deeply his philosophies and the workings of their community.

The wind was whistling harder now and the sky spat rain down on their dwelling, but the fire continued to crackle merrily from the pit. The fur Kaitlin laid on was of the softest quality, and the warmth of her husband's body made her nearly purr with happiness. When he began the next installment of his story, she listened with contented warmth.

"When I was fifteen winters, there were about ten of our band who traveled to the Valley of the Hills. This is where we Lakota gather for our dance. Each band camps together, but we all form one large circle surrounding the sacred location.

"On the first day, we prepare ourselves and the grounds. As with my vision quest, the participants begin with the cleansing rite: the *Inipi* ceremony. In addition, the whole area is purified by the supporters and holy men, for the dance is sacred. One man is chosen to cut a cottonwood tree down and bring it back to the ceremonial grounds. There may be several poles erected of the cottonwood, depending on the number of dancers.

"As part of the preparation, the poles are decorated and long leather straps are attached to the top. Each man would be assigned a pair of the cords. During the dance, the person's mentor keeps him energized and watches for signs of shock," Spirit Bear tried to explain.

"Why is this dance so dangerous?" Kaitlin asked, breaking in. "I realize you dance around the sacred cottonwood, but... I just don't understand. Do you catch the tree on fire?"

"The short version, *wastelaka*, is that each person to perform has each side of their chest punctured with bone hooks, just under each part of a pectoral muscle. That person must dance and pull back on the hooks until his skin and muscle break free. We have until sundown on the fourth day to tear the hooks from our bodies."

"What?" Kaitlin asked horrified. "Why? Why do people do this?"

"It is to show honor and daring. We celebrate the birth of vegetation to feed the buffalo who, in turn, provide for us. It is to earn a coup while the Earth breathes new life."

"What happens if your skin doesn't break free?" she asked, holding her breath.

"One of two things: Our mentor will add his weight when we pull back to help the skin give, or if the man is not free by sundown of the final day, we remove the hooks."

"Is that man still honored?" Kaitlin asked quietly. She could not imagine this horror, but to not break free for a Native man would be... shameful.

"*Tos*, any who agree to dance is honored. More coup is earned by breaking free, but you still earn coup by the process of the dance."

"How was it for you, *wastelaka*? Did you break free?"

Chief Spirit Bear

Chapter Thirteen
The Sun Dance: Fifteen Winters

The ten men from the Bear Claw Clan stood, evenly spaced, around one of the cottonwood poles. They wore only a breechclout. The sun was already hot on the morning of the dance, and after an *Inipi* ceremony, their bodies were thirsting for water.

Wandering Elk and Wind Walker were there to act as their holy men. In addition, each man performing also had an encourager; either a spiritual man or a friend who'd performed the rite in the past. Wonder Worker had not yet completed the dance, but he was considered an acting holy man. He was Spirit Bear's support.

Wandering Elk placed a few items at the foot of the Cottonwood, and so did the supporting members of the participants. The holy men put medicinal roots to help heal the puncture wounds and dried parts from the buffalo were also placed in the sun at the base of the sacred tree. Supporters placed packets of tobacco as prayers to *Wakantanka* to watch over the dancers.

Wandering Elk held up an elaborately carved pipe full of tobacco for all to see. "My people," he began. "Behold the Seven-Ceremonies Sacred Pipe given to the Lakota by the White Buffalo Woman!"

The men watched with intense focus. Their support people were given eagle bone whistles and fans made of the eagle's feathers. Wandering Elk lit the pipe and smoked it, passing it around to each man. Once everyone had smoked, he began to talk about the purpose of the Sun Dance.

"The Sun Dance was given to the Lakota as a time of renewal and rebirth. We rely on the buffalo that receives energy from the grasses and rains to sustain life. We sacrifice the blood of ourselves to feed the Earth to help the regeneration of our futures!" Wandering Elk proclaimed.

The men's voices raised in support of his words and in prayer to the Great Spirit. Eagle whistles were blown to add to the holy ritual. Wandering Elk began thanking the four directions, smoking his pipe while blowing smoke to indicate each. He praised and continued to blow smoke to the earth and *Wakantanka*.

"We also show our thankfulness to the buffalo, the Great Wonder, and *Wakantanka* by participating in this sacred ceremony," Wandering Elk continued.

More prayers, eagle flutes, and feathers were flapped. Next, Wind Walker arrived with a mammoth of a bison skull filled with sage. He stopped at every dancer and placed rings of sage on their heads, wrists, and ankles. He also gave the extra to the supporting men.

"Dancers, we begin!" Wandering Elk cried.

The elderly holy man walked to the first dancer standing in a circle around the cottonwood. Wind Walker stood beside him and handed the holy man a bone hook he'd secured to one of the thongs that attached it to the cottonwood. Wandering Elk pinched up some flesh on the left side of the man's chest and stabbed the sharpened fragment under the skin and part of the pectoral muscle.

As the process was performed, the warrior stood straight and strong, unflinching as he was pierced. The procedure was repeated on the right side. Then Wind Walker waved eagle feathers around the man while his supporter blew on the eagle flute whistle.

Each dancer had the same procedure repeated. Finally, they arrived at Spirit Bear's side. Wandering Elk's eyes crinkled a minute amount as he looked at the young man. Spirit Bear understood it to mean reassurance. Somehow the shaman knew he was afraid he'd show pain when pierced. He did not want to indicate any discomfort!

Spirit Bear did not flinch as the sharpened bone was driven through his flesh. In a sear of white heat, the needle was through. When it was over, he leaned back slightly against the piercing, testing the feel of the attachment.

When all were secured to the cottonwood, Wandering Elk directed them to shuffle a slow circle around him while keeping the tension on the hooks. Wandering Elk smoked more pipe and again, thanked the four directions, the Earth, and *Wakantanka* as Wind Walker waved the eagle wing over the participants. Eagle flutes were sounded along with prayer.

"Now, we begin the Sun Dance!" cried Wandering Elk once the men had completed the first circle.

Drums were sounded and eagle flutes accompanied. The men began a dance around the pole, facing the cottonwood, while leaning back against the hooks. It was a strange feeling for Spirit Bear. There was pain, yes. He felt the hooks pulling his flesh. The harder he pushed back against the line, the further his skin stretched.

When Spirit Bear looked down, he noticed the ropes hooked to his chest created hooded, bloody tents of skin. Sweat ran down his body and mingled with crimson trails. As the sun beat down on them mercilessly, the experience intensified.

On and on, the men danced with stomping feet. Hours crept by, but still, they kept making circles around the cottonwood as they sang prayers to the Great Spirit. With each movement of their feet, the men would throw themselves back to rip their skin.

Each pass would shorten the ropes a little. On occasion, a man would take a break. Some went around others, for each person danced to his own time although the external rhythm kept a steady beat.

Blood was now trailing onto the dirt; it blended in, adding a rust tinge to the earth. The dancers looked up at the sky to pay homage to the sun as it blazed down upon them. Partners continued to wave eagle feathers over the dancers and pipe on the flutes.

The heat, smoke, and lack of refreshments paired with the pain of pulling constantly against the bone hooks made Spirit Bear disoriented. One man went down on a knee. His partner lifted him back up and encouraged him to continue.

Spirit Bear lunged back and pain seared across his chest. He leaped back again, feeling a little unsteady, but with each rip, he came nearer to freedom. His upper body screamed with the white-hot heat that burned with every bit of progress made with the bone. For a moment, he believed it was actually on fire!

Spirit Bear saw the hunk of his flesh protrude as he pulled back yet again. Blood was bubbling from it, but he could see the white of the bone as it ripped. One hook was nearly freed! The dizzying circles and constant flute cries echoed in his head. It gave his performance a surreal quality.

At last, one hook broke free. A small piece of his flesh was attached. His smooth chest now contained a small crater of ripped flesh that oozed a steady trickle of blood. It blazed, but it was a pain that registered somewhere from the back of his mind.

"Look!" he heard Wonder Worker cry out. "Spirit Bear has one side free!"

Many voices raised in chant. Flutes and drums celebrated.

Another voice cried, "Black Snake is also starting to break free!"

Coups were being earned! The exhausted men seemed to find a second breath, encouraged by each success.

As each individual freed himself, he was praised with encouragement, prayer, and instruments. Right when the sun was nearing the horizon, Spirit Bear broke completely from his restraints. He stumbled back from the force of the lunge. Wonder Worker caught him before he crashed to the earth. Blood was running in rivulets down his abdomen,

Spirit Bear looked down and saw his chest wounds gaping open. The ripped flesh was raw and bloody. The angry punctures would make remarkable scars that would announce his bravery and daring to all.

He was very proud of his accomplishment! He was the first warrior to break free from the Sun Dance, and that was a huge feat. His worry about showing pain had melted away as he'd fought to break free from the tongs alongside his peers.

Spirit Bear looked up at Wonder Worker and beamed a bright smile. His friend returned his look with one of admiration and praise. With an animated face, the young shaman helped his friend back to his feet.

"Bring him to the healing tipi," Wandering Elk commanded.

As Wonder Worker helped Spirit Bear leave the Sun Dance, the young man saw a helper add his weight and pull back on Spotted Horse. One side of his friend ripped free. A small fountain of blood seemed to shoot forward in slow motion, but a cry of victory erupted from the warrior's mouth.

When Spirit Bear reached the relative shade of the hut, Wandering Elk treated his wounds. After instructing Wonder Worker on how to care for him, which included trickling small amounts of water into his mouth every fifteen minutes, the shaman returned to the other Sun Dancers.

Chapter Fourteen
Differences in Culture

Kaitlin was speechless. The Sun Dance seemed so barbaric to her. Some of the practices of these Native people appeared very crude, but others were very advanced. She wondered if she'd ever understand.

As Kaitlin processed her husband's story, she felt the weight of his gaze. She knew he was awaiting a response. She was shocked and appalled that these majestic people elected to maul themselves to help grass grow. However, she knew she had to come to terms with her feelings; she would never offend these proud people on purpose, especially the one she loved more than life.

Still, her mind turned to their child growing within her. Kaitlin was learning more about these wonderful but strangely savage people's beliefs and practices, and she understood that she'd have to subject her child to their ways. She was now one with the band; there would be no return to her more cultured way of life. The blonde woman knew there would be periods of violent training in the *Ojilaka's* upraising, especially if the baby were a man-child.

Finally, Kaitlin propped up on her elbow and examined her husband's sculpted chest. Her fingers lightly traced the star-shaped scars on either side of his pecs. At first, she would outline one and then softly trail across his chest to the other. He watched her but said nothing.

"It is hard for me to imagine this ceremony," she finally admitted. "It sounds so intense and spiritual."

"*Tos, wastelaka*. I know it is hard to understand why we warriors must prove ourselves," he agreed, "but there have even been *winyans* undertake the dance on occasion."

"Really?" Kaitlin asked.

"*Tos. Wakantanka* calls many to his service."

Kaitlin kept tracing his scars, first one and then the other.

"Did it hurt a lot?" she asked.

"It was a very intense ceremony," Spirit Bear replied softly. "*Tos*, it hurt, but the whole experience was… overwhelmingly spiritual. It is hard to explain."

"I cannot imagine," Kaitlin agreed.

"The heat, the pain, the constant whistle blowing, the cheering and prayer, it engulfs your senses so much so that there is nothing else like it. It was an honor to have been called to dance."

"As always, I am in awe of all that you do and are," Kaitlin said, hugging him. "I am so fortunate that the Great Spirit gave us to each other."

"*Tos*, my love, it is true! We are both very blessed."

The rain began to pick up tempo. Soon, it was slashing at the tipi. The wind, not to be outdone, hit at the barrier with growling force. Kaitlin rolled to her back. Her husband's hand returned to rest on her stomach.

"Every year, you have such adventure," Kaitlin said tenderly. "How did you ever endure it all?"

"It was expected," Spirit Bear said simply. "I did not know anything different."

Kaitlin knew that had to be accurate. She'd grown up in a whole different structure. It was hard to fathom what it would be like to know nothing else.

"Your men do not do anything to show their cunning and bravery?" Spirit Bear asked.

"*Hiya*, not to my knowledge," Kaitlin admitted. "White men compete, but it's all very safe and painless. The most they experience is anger from losing."

"That is something *I* cannot imagine," said Spirit Bear. "Most of our major rites involve blood of some sort. In addition, one loses power for anger displays."

It was true, Kaitlin knew. There were many examples of the differences of cultures between the two peoples. It seemed that only Kaitlin had this knowledge. She had no one to share it with, really; She didn't have anyone to help her understand their deep beliefs yet, but she was gaining in her comprehension the more she was exposed.

Kaitlin's brother, Bobby, had met these imposing people and was learning. He'd met and accepted her place in the Native society. He even respected them, Kaitlin suspected, more than their own people.

"I wish the ska, or white culture, was more honorable," Kaitlin said finally. "But then again, we'd never have met."

Spirit Bear's eyes darkened at this revelation.

"I do not believe that is true," he said, looking at her intently. "We were meant to be, and *Wakantanka* would have found a way."

Kaitlin nodded. She couldn't, wouldn't imagine a life without him.

"I love you, *Woniya Mato*. With all my heart!"

"And I love you, *wastelaka*, with every ounce of me."

Kaitlin was contemplative. After her mind had absorbed the Sun Dance ritual, it was still curious about the bear fight. In her mind, even as serious as the Sun Dance seemed to be, it was nothing in comparison to what she imagined fighting a bear in hand-combat would be.

"When did you decide to fight the bear?" she blurted.

Spirit Bear smiled instantly. He'd wondered what was going through her mind. He should have known it was more questions.

"The summer after the Sun Dance, I finally felt prepared," he replied.

"So you were sixteen winters?"

The chief nodded.

"How did you know you were ready?" Kaitlin couldn't imagine ever being prepared.

"When we pray and meditate, we are given a sign from our totem when the time is right. I did not speak with my spiritual bear, but he allowed me to catch a glimpse of him one morning. I knew he was telling me that it was time."

"Where did you go? How did you choose?"

"We are aware of our environments, and we knew where a male had resided for winter. He would be a perfect candidate, so we went to his lair."

Kaitlin sucked in a breath. "You fought a bear as it was coming out of hibernation?"

"We watched it for a week or two to allow his senses to recover from winter. When the bear become alert but are still lean yet hungry, they are the most dangerous."

Kaitlin's hand stilled. She was terrified for him even though he was right before her.

"The first bear I fought was when snow still blanketed the lands."

"The *first* bear?" Kaitlin sucked in a breath.

"*Tos*. I was instructed to fight both black and grizzly bears for my right to become war chief."

110

Chapter Fifteen
Bear Power: Sixteen Winters

BLACK BEAR

Oglala warriors had been watching the bear cave since mid-February, anticipating the animal's emergence. Finally, nearing the end of the month, the black beast appeared into the brilliant sunshine.

The ground was a shimmering glaze on top of a soft stuffing of powder. Trees were encased in crystal, and the crackling of branches and sounds of ice falling punctuated the background. The bear groggily snuffled the air. The men watched in silence as it lifted its shiny black nose to try to locate the smell of meat.

Spirit Bear had killed a small deer and placed it strategically close to the lair. Normally, a bear emerged from its den in a state of sleepy exhaustion. It took a few weeks for the animal to build up energy and become fully aware. Spirit Bear wanted the black beast to return to strength faster than it would have otherwise.

After eating, the bear dragged the remains to the cave's entrance and scraped a bit of snow over the carcass. Then it returned to the cavern to digest its meal. Spirit Bear continued to feed the animal for several weeks before believing the liveliness had been restored to the powerful creature.

The future war chief spent the days before the battle with his totem in prayer and meditation. He cleansed and isolated himself in a cave near his village. Upon his return, Spirit Bear ate and drank to replenish his energy before undertaking the most challenging of his fights yet. A band of *Cante Tinza,* along with Wandering Elk and Wonder Worker, would accompany him to the bear's lair.

On the day of the encounter, Spirit Bear applied the paint he would adopt as a war chief. First, he drew a black line horizontally across his face beginning high on his cheekbones and traveling across his nose. A second horizontal red line underscored the first. He'd chosen the colors of his trademark feathers, the red hawk. The three red vertical lines on both sides of his cheeks indicated the power of the bear.

Spirit Bear strapped two of his favored hunting knives to his waist as well as his war tomahawk. He would need every weapon to fight the bear's natural ones. The warrior took a deep breath, held it, then exhaled. He sent one last prayer to *Wakantanka* before going to find his men.

"*Tokas*, I am ready," he said to the friends that would accompany him.

He flashed a confident smile which they returned. Normally, his friends would have engaged in banter with him, but it was a rare thing when a warrior was called to fight a bear in hand combat, and Spirit Bear was to undertake two. No one wanted to disrupt the connection he'd established with the spirit world. It could mean the difference between life and death.

When they arrived at the bear's lair, Spirit Bear went directly to the spot the beast had secured his last meal. The animals were highly protective of their food. Nothing would make it angrier than to make it think its sustenance was in danger.

It didn't take long for the bear to become aware that it had company. The war party had hidden. Spirit Bear made a stand against the black, and it came charging with an enraged bellow.

The animal barreled down upon him! At the last second, Spirit Bear jumped behind the mound of debris covering the carcass. The beast was moving at a fast clip and had difficulty stopping quickly. Spirit Bear had counted on this. He drew his knife, and in a flash, he made a long gash in the bear's shoulder.

The mammal screamed in pain and confusion. It jerked its head toward the wound, and saliva slung from its open jaws. When the bear reared up, the wound gaped open, exposing bone and gristle; Spirit Bear had made the stab count.

Blood was beginning to fill the gash. It spurted down its leg and trailed into the dirt. The enraged bear thundered loudly. It slashed out at the man with its four daggers.

Again, Spirit Bear was ready. He swung his tomahawk against the bear's swipe. There was a sickening crack of bone on the blade, and the bear bellowed again. The sound seemed to reverberate through the hills.

The animal turned, standing on three legs. The right paw dangled at an odd angle. It lowered its head, and its eyes seemed to shoot red fire. The roar that exploded from its throat would have scared any man. The beast's open mouth exposed long, white canines that appeared to be over two inches long.

Spirit Bear calmly walked out from his cover to face his totem.

"*Mato*, I am sorry to sacrifice your life, but the Great Spirit Bear has promised me your strength."

The bear focused its livid gaze on the warrior and charged. For a moment, Spirit Bear disappeared; he was covered by black, shaggy fur. The *Cante Tinza* held its breath, unsure of what to do. The bear awkwardly rose again and seemed to hover a moment. A bloody man was holding it up. Spirit Bear threw the beast down and its large head lolled to the side in death.

The group that accompanied the youthful man charged to his side. Spirit Bear held up a hand and said, "I am fine, *kolas*. The blood you see is the bear's. When he charged at me, he could not outthink his anger. I was able to open his throat with my knife."

GRIZZLY BEAR

In the weeks that followed, Spirit Bear rested and recovered. Grizzlies typically awakened two to four weeks after their smaller black relatives. The brethren of warriors were on-board to help their future chief find the den of a grizzly.

Finally, a very large male was located. The group had to travel quite a bit further in order to reach the animal's territory. After preparation similar to that of the black bear, Spirit Bear was ready to fight his final totem war. Due to the animal's size, Spirit Bear was allowed a shield as well as his hand weapons.

The grizzly was enormous. Although it was still lean from his hibernation time, the beast was close to a thousand pounds. The animal didn't need much provoking; he was spoiling for a fight. It saw the warrior standing in his domain and took it for what it was – a challenge.

Spirit Bear stood, ready, before the quickly approaching beast. Chief Takes Chances stood by his side, invisible to all but Spirit Bear. He said, "Remember *Cinks*, it is good to have fear in your heart but not in your actions. It will keep you alive."

All of a sudden, a white essence of a smaller bear jumped inside the warrior. Spirit Bear knew it was the brother he'd defeated. Now, the essence of his totem was within him. They would join their minds so that Spirit Bear could better predict his foe's movements. Together, they would defeat the grizzly!

The roar of the charging bear was deafening. The ground was being ripped apart as the heavy animal closed the distance.

"I will block his vision when he comes close," his father said. "You jump up and the bear will guide your feet."

When the grizzly reached Spirit Bear, he ran to meet him and jumped, trusting in Chief Takes Chances's instructions. His foot somehow landed on the beast's forehead and propelled him into the air. Spirit Bear did a backflip over the mad animal. While upside down, he was able to bring first blood. His knife ripped flesh with the bear's rush.

The behemoth bellowed in rage. He turned and came again. Blood was flowing down the animal's sides. Spirit bear withdrew his tomahawk and prepared his shield. He braced himself for the hit.

When the grizzly met Spirit Bear, he deflected by pushing out with the shield and swinging the axe. The resounding crack was drowned by a murderous roar. The bear bit the shield and flung it roughly.

Spirit Bear found himself airborne. He hadn't let go of the shield when the bear hurled it. When he landed, he rolled and was back on his feet in a flash. The bear was right there, snapping at the protection. He swung the tomahawk again, and it stuck in the top of the bear's head.

The grizzly stood to his full height, roaring deeply in confusion and pain. Spirit Bear took advantage of the slash of time. He took his long hunting blade and cut open the bear's abdomen. A few of the grizzly's shiny intestines were visible. In mere moments, the bear began to gush blood.

When the beast came down, his claws ripped at Spirit Bear. The animal's weapons cut into Spirit Bear's thigh and rolled him. Again, the warrior was able to spring up.

The bear was weakening. It still had a lot of power left, and it made another attempt to stop his opponent. Crimson rivers were streaming down its head and into its eyes. Spirit Bear jumped onto the beast's back and shimmied up its shoulders.

The grizzly bawled furiously. He lunged and bucked, trying to dislodge his rider. Spirit Bear clung to his wet fur. Finally, as the bear's motions slowed as it weakened, Spirit Bear was able to loosen his hold enough to brandish his knife. He held the blade high then drove down with a blinding force.

The weapon was buried deeply beside the axe into the bear's head. With a loud *ooof* of rushed air, the bear collapsed and ceased to move.

"Thank you, *mato*, for the gift of your life and power," Spirit Bear said rising from the animal's shoulders. "In appreciation, I will make an offering in the name of your sacrifice. *Woniya Mato* has spoken!"

The *Cante Tinza* erupted from their concealment with whoops and loud undulations. They lifted Spirit Bear onto their backs, crying in joy and triumph. The fight was totally unbelievable if they hadn't seen it for themselves.

"That was impressive!" Yellow Feather declared. "I have never seen such a fight!"

"*Tos*, and we will never see one such as this again," agreed Sky Warrior. "I am honored to follow you, *Woniya Mato*!"

Lone Wolf said, "You have earned the name, *mato*, my friend!"

Finally, Wonder Worker said, "My brother, please let me see to your wound. It would not do to let it go too long without cleaning it."

Spirit Bear, after the cheering had died down, allowed himself to be treated by the medicine man.

GREAT SPIRIT BEAR:

"Spirit Bear, I am very proud of you, *Cinks,*" the great white bear said. "You have done as I have instructed. You trusted blindly in my coaching. You have mastered the power of the bear. He will serve you well."

"Thank you, Father. I am glad you stood by my side," the future war chief said.

"Do you see why I told you to fight the black bear first?" the Great Bear asked.

"*Tos*. Without his power to help me, I could not have won against the grizzly."

The great bear nodded, his brilliance was evidenced in the white light but also from the feeling of power and purity it exuded.

"Thank you for finding me worthy," Spirit Bear finally said. He felt overwhelmed with gratitude.

"You were chosen many moons ago, my son. You will lead an honorable life. It may not be easy, but you are the man your nation needs."

Spirit Bear was so overcome with the honor that he couldn't respond.

"Lead your people well. Goodbye, *Cinks*. Until we meet again."

Chapter Sixteen
Calm

"Spirit Bear! I have never heard such an amazing story!" Kaitlin breathed. She sat in amazement of her husband's exciting life. Her golden eyes were wide with wonder.

He nodded agreement; the warrior realized, more than she, what a reward it truly was.

"I will never completely stop worrying, but your story will help my mind to calm when you are away in war. It really helps to know that your father and two bears help you fight!" Kaitlin's wonder was evident in her breathy tone.

"The honor is endless," Spirit Bear agreed. "My spirit totems and guide paired with my council brothers are, as of yet, an undefeatable combination. One must stay humble so that *Wakantanka* continues to see our worthiness."

"It is so hard to believe that you fought two bears, you *alone* and by *hand*, and were not mauled. All you got was this as a reminder!" her hand went his thigh to finger yet more of his scars.

"I see it now!" she exclaimed upon closer examination.

"See what, *wastelaka*?" her husband asked curiously.

"Your war paint! Your scar is somehow three lines instead of four!"

Spirit Bear laughed. "I suppose you are right, my wife. My war paint was on my face before I was marked, but now I see the coincident as well!"

"Maybe your spirit bear knew and had the grizzly mark you so," she breathed in awe, "so that your war paint and your mark would match?"

"*Tos*. I *am* marked, as *Wakantanka* told me I would be. He revealed that this would happen in order to merge our souls so that I could harness the power of the bear."

"So your paint is the symbol of your youthful name, Red Hawk, given to you by your father, and by the power of your totem, the spirit bear, right?"

"*Tos*, very good, my wife. I wanted to honor my father and the long line of war chiefs in my blood. I also am named for the Great Spirit of the Bear, also reflected in my paint."

"It's so very clever!" Kaitlin agreed. "I am so grateful, all over again, that *you* are my husband!"

She hugged him as closely as her protruding stomach would allow. Spirit Bear laughed at her enthusiasm.

"I assume that you were named war chief soon after the grizzly's defeat?" she asked.

"*Tos*. I recovered from the mark first, but then the community was ready to celebrate! They waited until my seventeenth winter day."

"Your day of birth is when you became war chief?"

"Tos."

"What an honor! I cannot wait to hear!" Kaitlin said breathlessly.

"The ceremony was like most others," Spirit Bear said. "So I will begin by telling you of my induction."

"Thank you, my chief! I really appreciate you sharing so deeply with me! I love you so much!"

Chapter Seventeen
War Chief: Seventeen Winters

"And now, my people!" Chief Storm Cloud began, "After the new warriors' induction, our protectors need a leader!"

The crowd roared in approval.

"We have gone many winters without an acting war chief," he said. "Finally, the man we've been watching for years has agreed it is time!"

Chief Tracking Dog said, "We know that Spirit Bear is a young man. He is young for the *Cante Tinza*, and he is young for a chief, but *Wakantanka* knows better than we mortal men!"

The multitude was deafening with support.

"His father, Chief Takes Chances, our then-acting-war-chief, was taken from us when Spirit Bear was nine winters. Eight years later, we find his son worthy of that title." Chief Storm Cloud held an elaborate war lance.

"Spirit Bear," called Wandering Elk. "Come forward."

Spirit Bear walked proudly forward. He was dressed in mahogany finery with intricate quill designs of turquoise, white, red, and black. The leggings were fringed as was his tunic.

"Would the people enjoy a telling of this man's feats?" Lone Wolf asked, facing the throng.

The crowd screamed and whistled their desire.

The chiefs told of Spirit Bear's trail of feats. They spoke of his first coup when he defeated Night Hawk and of his induction into the *Cante Tinza*.

"Spirit Bear was the earliest winter ever known to enter our warrior's society," Chief Storm Cloud announced.

"He was also young when he honored *Wakantanka* with the sacred Sun Dance!" Wandering Elk cried.

"And now, we will reenact the bear combats!" Lone Wolf announced.

Sky Warrior wore the black bear's skin. He and Spirit Bear began the tale for the community. The crowd learned about feeding the animal upon its emergence from the cave. Then the two men recreated the actual fight.

Near the ending of the 'fight', Sky Warrior charged Spirit Bear and flew the bear skin upon him. Spirit Bear fell back and then raised the animal's skin up and threw it off of him, indicating the transfer of power and the animal's death. The gathering went wild.

Next, when the warrior fought the grizzly, Yellow Feather was the bear. Right before the huge creature charged, Sky Warrior, wearing the black bear skin, ran to stand beside Spirit Bear as did Lone Wolf with paint on his face similar to Chief Takes Chances.

The throng gasped then held its breath. Startled cries erupted when Chief Takes Chances distracted the grizzly's vision and then the black bear skin became one with Spirit Bear. Never before had the community witnessed the first strike in the killing of a grizzly, and never before had it occurred from a backflip over a charging beast.

Finally, the great animal lay still in death. The community began yelling praises to the Great Spirit and thanking him for giving them such a powerful leader. Not many could wield the power of bears at their beckon and also have help from a spirit.

Chief Storm Cloud waited in respectful silence to allow the community to absorb what just occurred. Then he made an announcement.

"Spirit Bear, please come forth."

The young, powerful man did so.

"On this day of your birth, seventeen winters later, will you accept gifts from you powerful totems?" Wandering Elk asked.

"*Tos.*"

Spirit Bear leaned forward to accept the bear claw and teeth *wanapin*. Wonder Worker slipped it over his head with a huge, proud smile.

The symbolic necklace was a double row of gifts from both of his totems. The smaller, inner strand contained canines and claws from the black bear while the longer one held those of the grizzly. There were red hawk feathers present as well as intermingling stones of red, black and other earthy tones.

"You are the only man in this band to ever fight two bears and harness their power," Wandering Elk said.

"And walk away with only a mark," added Chief Tracking Dog. Chief Storm Cloud tamped the lance on the ground for effect.

The *Cante Tinza* began to circle the men in the center. They all withdrew their knives. This was not an initiation into the warrior group, this was electing their chief!

Spirit Bear took out his long hunting knife as well. He made a cut on either side of his shoulders and held his knife to the sky.

He cried out, "*Wakantana!*"

The whole ceremony stilled for a few moments in respect. Then, the shaman broke the silence.

"Do you, men of the *Cante Tinza*, elect Spirit Bear as your leader?"

All the men, as one, raised their hunting knives. Then they all cut their arms in unison as their new chief had done. Afterwards, they lifted their knives once more toward the heavens.

Raising their voices together, the men cried, "*Wakantanka* has blessed us with the man we've been waiting for our whole lives. Only the Bear Claw Clan can be led by a bear!"

Wonder Worker came out, painted in white. He had a bone and feather mask covering his upper face. As he danced around the men, he blew on an eagle flute and waved eagle fathers around the warriors. Wandering Elk smoked the pipe and blew smoke onto Warrior Bear. Then Chief Storm Cloud offered Spirit Bear the chieftain lance. Spirit Bear accepted.

With the blood was oozing down his arms, Spirit Bear cried, "My people, I am beyond honored! My warriors, friends, and family of the Bear Claw Clan, hear my humble words: I will do my best, in all manners, to lead you and protect you. I will give my life for you. I will not take our people in to war lightly.

Wakantanka and the spirit of the bears guide and protect me as I will you. Thank you for this honor!"

The crowd went wild! They surged forward and congratulated all the leaders. Then the feast and dancing began.

Chief Spirit Bear

Chapter Eighteen
More Respect

"What an honor!" Kaitlin cried. "Oh, *Woniya Mato*! I am so proud of you and all that you represent! You've achieved so much and at such an early age! What a past to shape who you are today!"

Spirit Bear smiled at his wife's reaction. "Thank you, *Mazaska Zi Ista*. It pleases me that I did not shock you with my experiences."

"Oh," she laughed. "I did not say I am not surprised. You are an astonishing man in many ways, but they are all good! I am just happy that you chose me from all of those that you could have."

"There was no other choice, my wife. *Wakantanka* knew and brought you to me. He only had to parade bears in front of me numerous times before I finally caught on."

Kaitlin laughed at his revere and humor. It sounded like happy bells tinkling around them.

"You wear so many hats and do them all so well," she continued. "You are loving husband, respected ruler, and very scary warrior all wrapped in one. How do you do it?" she breathed.

Spirit Bear considered and said, "It is not planned, it just happens. I believe the will of *Wakantanka* guides my spirit for whatever role I must assume."

"You are perfect, *wastelaka*!" she said softly.

"It is you who is perfect!" he argued.

"Together, we will make good parents," Kaitlin exclaimed against his neck as she snuggled closer to him. He wrapped his arm around her, a steel band of warm metal against her skin.

"The best," he agreed, smiling brilliantly.

References:

Spirit Quest:

http://aktalakota.stjo.org/site/News2?page=NewsArticle&id=8672

Sun Dance:

http://aktalakota.stjo.org/site/News2?page=NewsArticle&id=8668

And

Zelitch, .Jeffrey"The Lakota Sun Dance" *Expedition Magazine* 13.1 (1970): n. pag. *Expedition Magazine*. Penn Museum, 1970 Web. 26 Feb 2019 <http://www.penn.museum/sites/expedition/?p=2163>

Chief Spirit Bear

More from Sheri Chapman:

My website:
https://prayerpawpuppies.wixsite.com/authorsherichapman/books

Books

Wild Passion *(Book 1 of the Passion series – historical romance)*
Dove and Dragon Publishing
Wild Passion is COMING TO THE MOVIE SCREEN!!!
(It will be PG13 and renamed "Captive Heart")
*preproduction finished
Passions of the Heart *(Book 2 of the Passion series – NEWLY RELEASED: 2019)*
Dove and Dragon Publishing
"Eyes with No Soul" *(YA paranormal suspense) – Dove and Dragon Publishing*

BOOKS coming in 2020 *(by Dove and Dragon Publishing):*
***Werewolves Don't Like Green Beans** - (YA, Book 1 of Wolves Unchained)*
***Protectors of the People** - (YA, Book 2 of Wolves Unchained)*
***A Killer, Revisited** – (A Sci-fi detective story)*
***The Other Side of Privileged** – (A modern day Cinderella story)*

Anthologies coming in 2019
Just a Drop: Vampire Anthology: **"The Vampire Prophecy"** –
Wild Dreams Publishing
Calendar Themed Anthologies (Volume 1 Fantasy/Paranormal):
"The Magic of the Leprechaun"
Wild Dreams Publishing

Calendar Themed Anthologies (Volume 2 Romance): (HOT)
"The Chrysalis: A Modern-Day Medusa Story" — *Wild Dreams Publishing*
Calendar Themed Anthologies (Volume 3 Dark/Horror):
"Predatory Evil" — *Wild Dreams Publishing*